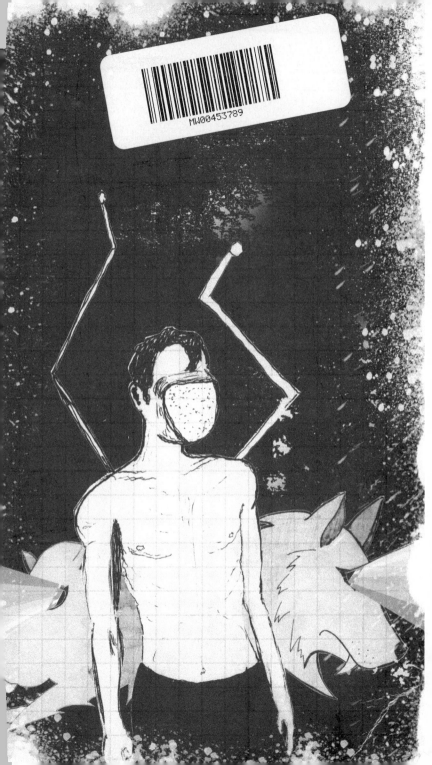

Copeland Valley Press

© Gary J. Shipley, 2013

Published in America by Copeland Valley Press

www.copelandvalley.com

Typeset in Janson

Design ©Matthew Revert

Art ©William Pauley III

ISBN: 978-0-9871561-8-1

Extracts from this work have been published in the following places: Dirty : Dirty: an anthology of dirty writing (Jaded Ibis Press), and Horror Sleaze Trash.

Dreams of Amputation

Gary J. Shipley

Men are deceived in the recognition of what is obvious, like Homer who was the wisest of all Greeks. For he was deceived by boys killing lice, who said: what we see and catch we leave behind; what we neither see nor catch we carry away.

Heraclitus

He wakes in a container, head like a sawn circuit, throat rattling like a battery cage, Dock Code Report flashing tortured symbols from the wall screen: the amp's back.

The hooks are in. It takes seconds: brain disease, murder patrols, the melded noises of hell infused – to those in the know – with the whispered portent of some sub-notional virginplot.

The signs are good so far: there are others, their forebears, hybrid corpse mechanisms threshing out a path. But he knows to slow down, been caught out too many times before – always the interpretive flaws. Dangers there already: on the first drop signs of infection, soul-mass discrepancies and viral chokers. All stuff he'd come across before, but each of them a threat if left to spread.

He stands up, eyes locked to the screen, gut on the make, toes curling into the cold ochre soles of his feet. A dose of anti-quake in his scalp and within seconds the cranial tremors are petering out. Laced with the alchemic algorithms of its own imma-terial rebirth, his body's time is up and it knows it. He shambles over to the chair and opens up the day's new tag lines.

First one out he'd put down as fried. The quasi-Broca zone appeared to have been obliterated and he'd despaired through into panic. He was pinned down for days, unable to move, held fast by what he'd witnessed. The answer came to him all at once: voided circuits in the ArcFas bundle. That amp'd taken the germ with him, and his task was to extract some semblance of sense from the mutant spoor of his disappearing.

Airworms cut through the capsule on their early morn-ing run, their insatiable, toothless hunger serving as a filter for his weary lungs. Red beads in the screen: his eyes starting to bleed. He wipes them dry and pulls down his goggles, adjusts the backlighting and disappears, making way for the words, the frenzied architecture of his future-in-waiting. Input procedures and mainframe anomaly tests already running, and if there's any-thing new to find he'll beat them to it, he always does. And if he comes up blank, he'll propagandize his own existence to move on.

He hears the lid clunk shut on the dump-tube outside, the soulless whine of a Spectre-Mule lost in retro-servitude. The lights dim momentarily. He looks up at his windows, a response he recognizes as both archaic and masturbatory. He has them set to night-sky-no-stars, the closest setting to off he could find. They could be anywhere; the possible views innumerable for the sole purpose of concretizing space. It's an old dupe system – classic thought-waste mechanics – making earlier addiction schemes appear light-hearted, casual: his very own digital vampire ready to suck every last ounce of blood-time, leaving nothing behind but a body-shaped hole and every strident inch of its disquiet.

The repetition-streamer tabulates with the attention to detail – read automated glee – of the habitual sex-murderer, pattern-dressing chaos with the lifeless and unworldly eyes of deep-water fish. This is the corpse city dream of all his darkly ascetic brethren, ready to grind themselves into dust for the abstract escapology of ultimate form – their paradise on stilts. The black and jointless block-world is almost indistinguishable from the world that is taken for all its possibilities at once, but somewhere between the two there lies ultimate form, the goal, the catalyst for years of rot and gored hope. Hope. One should live without, they were told all that dead time back, and many did, and all decomposed on the bars of days of nights and nature's finest lies.

He sluices down his morning HB pill, appeasing the acids in his gut, conning the body into thinking it's sustained and so sustaining – biology made theoretics. All those old-time prophecies of pills replacing food came good: flesh reduced to the realization of its code. This is a glimpse of the way out, an early scam that gifted abstraction its new skin, making it conceptually visible, revealing the hyperreality of its existence to those still able to look.

Stretched bleep, light-burst, turn to screen 2: another container-jacking in progress. An unblinking eye on each screen: the terror of the old, the terror of the new, the grume of emotive function paralleling the encrypted theorems of hypothetical synthesis. Flash message. Diagnosis: remote reprogramming of Airworm diet from dirt to human tissue.

For a second or two there is the man, on his feet reaching for the back of his chair with his right hand, and then the dance of the vanishing begins: the flailing honeycombed limbs, naked bone glinting through a blood fog, burrowed organs hovering in the air like bloated dust particles, and so it goes until worm-holed meat and bone give way to empty space and the closing disinterment of faecal matter; eaten free of its fleshy coat it drops to the floor – a signature.

Whirling letters of code, RNA, DNA, phosphate bases, enzyme spatters, chromosomes, proteins, sequences, striped rods of mitochondria, the jig of genetic disclosure, cytoplasm, hormones, membranes, starburst nerve impulses, the fluid capering of cells, neurones, synapses, myelin sheaths, serotonin crystals, glucose sprays, the airborne foxtrot of fibres, dendrites, axons, thermoreceptors, nebulized nerve dots, spinal fluid secretions, Ranvier nodes… The fuzz of atoms, ions and isotopes, protons, neutrons, electron clouds, nuclei, photons, baryons, mesons, quarks… The mists of consciousness failing their abstract integer…

Dreams of Amputation

Screen down: show over.

The only faces he sees are of the dead and the soon to be dead. He's forgotten what a genuine smile looks like. If he was to approximate one from memory, he'd be forced to construct it in his head out of the grimaces of the perishing, and the curling pink brume of floating blood.

How quickly they disintegrate. Numbers of would-be amputees dwindling, and every time a new one goes they watch and turn the spurs in on themselves, the space they occupy quaking, losing confidence, every mind cleansing itself of the latest depletion to eventually regroup. But he's held rock-still by the report flooding his left eye, the abstract dream driving superordinate rivets through his fading humanity. He'll fall prey to the Reconstructionists, or he'll escape their listless fuck-hole of a world forever, but what he won't do is allow his fear to assist them. Instead, he'll submerge himself in the as-yet-unseeing eyes of his abstract fetus, clinging tighter still to every coded beat of its unborn heart.

Every time one manages to get away from their bunker, through the paradigmatic concreta and into the hinterlands of mereological function, they widen the path a little for those that follow. But at the same time each risks fissuring his consciousness forever, carved down the middle like some amoebic sexgame. Each time one goes through quantities of data fuse, connections sever, a good part of them left behind. When his time comes there will be none of it, no thought of retraction, no care for remanifestation; the next time there'll be nobody around to monitor it: his transmigration will be complete and any second thoughts will fry on exit.

The Sangraal of non-spatial consciousness is scrawling its digitized entrails across his eyes, its secrets and pathways un-making themselves like the ends of frayed twine. His attention wanes and the hollows move in; it's the same for all of them. There are those who have made friends with the dreary empti-ness of everything, worshipping at its snickering altar day and night; lost to themselves and the vacillations of hope, they find a kind of meaning in meaninglessness, actively pursuing its deadening voice for fear of hearing nothing at all. There was a time when failings of life were blamed for these tired rat-tlings of the soul, but now it's the accepted lifestyle of many who, sick with fighting it off, just went ahead and claimed it for their own. It is, they argue, the natural accompaniment to our environment, its fearful futures, isolation, confinement, and restricted potential for exercise, concentration and sleep. They spend their time trying to convert others, helping them to see that their struggle with pointlessness is pointless. They call themselves the harbingers of human truth, and wear their self-prescribed gloom like a kiss-me-quick hat. For all their ex-hausted possibilities they are still amongst his greatest enemies. None of these bleating sirens can be allowed to infect his unen-cumbered hereafter with their want for yielding. And although he has blocked all intercourse with their kind, this has not dissuaded them from trying to hack in and save him from all im-probabilities of desire. They'll keep going until he goes, and if he doesn't cover his tracks they'll follow him. They've trained their eyes to cut arrows out the unlighted, arrows that only converts see or want to see, and so to them his absence will be nothing. These ghouls of illogic are without fear, remorse or humour, their resolve unyielding; with the bared bleached teeth of salesmen these red-eyed missionaries of melancholy hawk despair to anyone still capable of scraping together a fu-ture. Impossible to defeat, the only hope is to be out of earshot by the time these charismatic doom-merchants find their way into your system.

On the other end of the scale, and yet another cause for concern, are The Love Militia: soft-hearted and soft-headed en-thusiasts of the great biological con. Undeterred by its flimsy expansion, its demand for mind-breaking servitude, and the ob-vious absence of any appropriate objects, they go all-out to keep the poor threadbare thing alive. And the ends to which they are prepared to go... Oh what ends, what ends... Most spend their time locked in the static embrace of love scripts; back and forth go the tired-arsed laments on longing and unfulfilled desire: "If only we could..." "How I long to..." "I'd never let go..." And then there are the delusions of making do: "This is the purest, finest love, untainted by proximity..." "Your words touch me in a way your body never could..." "But aren't we together in all ways that matter?..." If he could afford to laugh he would; he'd never be able to stop; he'd chuckle, hoot and snort himself into a six-foot rictus.

('RSS ALERT': A residual sorrow sample, first of the exit bugs. That miserable dirt gets in everywhere, hiding itself between the lines, waiting for the optimum configuration to give it a nudge. Before long the entire script is infected. He sets about putting the quarantine procedure in place. Diagnosing the threat level and targeting the exact source takes time, but once sectioned off it can exact no further damage.)

Wake screen up and falling. Amp's disintegration flashing back. Back from nowhere, brain infused with whispers of hell, techniques born from interpretive flaws. The artificer lives on infection. His porridge stretching to the gelid undersides of his feet. His flesh eating into the chair through his clothes and into his voided circuits. Satiation is death. Murderous red tears reflected on the inside of his goggles. Soulless whine of a restarted Spectre-Mule. The windows a response to the possibility of a view, some light-hearted machinery veiling the hecatomb, their repetitions digitized into the abstract dust of some ultimate form, a black rot living off decomposing strangers, soul scraps united into a spectral consumer of unattended selves cross-wired on the screen before his eyes: a lunatic theatre of solidified consciousnesses, theoretics made meat. Trickery's unblinking progress sending and receiving messages to and from remote corners of the globe – flailing worm-holed bodies and the wool of abstract faces approximated from a conglomerated parasite clearing their minds with city dreams of submerged truths hidden in a fetus yet to be conceived. Data scrawls across his eyes, lost to itself and all individualized meaning, and so this orchestrated glyphics of the soul claims him for its own.

She sits in the passenger seat of the car in a lay-by on the edge of the desert. The dunes in the distance heave and flicker like the clouds of an electrical storm laid across the horizon. Her door is open, and her long brown legs extend free of the car, her heels buried in wiry tufts of brown grass. Her hair is gathered in a ponytail that drapes lazily over her bare right shoulder. Her white, strapless summer dress is covered in hundreds of tiny blue birds frozen in mid-flight; between them they exhaust all 360 points of departure, forever threatening to collide into one another, with only a few having their way clear for escape. The sun illuminates her legs while her face remains hidden in the shade.

She leans forward, pulls her sunglasses down onto the end of her nose, and smiles. Her teeth are white, fulgent and even, her eyes dark and mischievous.

"Are you spying on me?" she asks.

She places her hands on her knees, closes her eyes and inclines her face toward the sun.

"I want you to bring me here again," she says; "I want to come here again soon."

She slides her sunglasses back up over her eyes, and leans back into the relative cool of the car.

There are Paradoxites outside. He hears their shuffling horde long before they start their trademark attempts at entry. By the time they get to the container door he'll have his defences up. They run through their repertoire of techniques, hoping to find a sucker to devour, someone that'll let them in on a promise and never be in a position to let them out again. The Paradoxites redefine contrary; the square of opposition is their playground: they have a toe in every pie and more coats than an Alaskan scaghead. Their material form is unstable: all things to all men and many things to many men at any one time. Each one nervous, identity-starved, lunatic, streaming, sycophantic, cutthroat, cartoonish, strobic – each one a puddle of stirred time. If they manage to gain access to a container the result is truly extraordinary, impossible to grasp and yet so absorbing it has been known to produce prolonged bouts of psychosis in the unprepared observer.

Dreams of Amputation

A gang-rape is a teary-eyed declaration of love, a harmless poetry recital complete with nerve-addled enunciation and self-conscious fidgets; a brutal beating is at once a nursing to health, a murder a frenzied resuscitation, an anal fisting the gentle hair-harvest of apes... Ripped apart and sewn up, ripped apart and sewn up, ripped apart and sewn up, until all that is left behind is stitched cotton soaked in human tissue. Many have doubted their existence – and who could blame them; after all, they are at worst half-right – thinking them to be nothing more than a bogeyman device to keep them all tucked up in private space. He believes, has seen their work in all its impossible glory.

He recites from the manifesto:

"If you want to see that nothing is left for us here, see the empty physicality of flesh made plastic and metal, the care-worn snarls of the young; look at the world that cannot look back – dirty rags black with human history. Nothing is left but the scared little corners that we've painted ourselves into. If you want to see, then first listen to the dreary death tolls of universal knowness, the heavy handed wrist-slash of completeness, that once distant beacon, that unholy brain-whisk: a noble goal for a man to find and leave behind for countless other men who would not thank him for it, who could not thank him for it, who should not thank him for it. Look at the blunted pick-axes devoured by rust and worm that could not put so much as a dent in that legacy of doomy slack. If you want to be sure, read those empty circles of diamond-snotted crust, our souls forced through fetid miles of intestinal tubing, men and women rotting on the vine. See the sky that is hidden from you opening up for an ant's unfocused dreams, see the terror-card of inactivity, and the blossom in dead trees; see the unstructured sadness of those that posture their lives into insignificance. If you still need convincing, you are already dead in all ways that matter; if you still need convincing, you are the disease I'm running from."

They're still out there – even if they're not. His successfully shutting them out means that they are also in there with him, in his head, torturing syllogistic premises into quivering submission. If he was to let them in would they then be outside? Is that what they want him to think, so also what they don't want him to think? These are the kind of traps they get you with if you aren't careful enough to care.

He can still remember the days when intellectuals of all persuasions scrambled for new ideas, scientists for unanswered questions, poets and writers for new ways to laugh and cry, artists for new materials or fresh approaches to the old ones. They fought for so long; they couldn't stop themselves. The art of criticism died when its practitioners set up home in the trenches, and found themselves unable to even so much as peek out over the top. These were more distracted and so happier times. But looking back on them was like watching a child fight quicksand.

And still the sense of incompleteness persisted; and what a sorry sight, those severed hands at prayer, those nomads reaching for a home.

Dreams of Amputation

All systems are running smoothly. No contact from the others: they maintain network silence unless there's a problem. They only hear from one another if the news is bad. The latest amp has not failed them. The reports are almost screeching their salvation. This time he'll leave the brain-clamp on: no point duplicating when he has the hardware in place. There'll be nothing much left when he goes. Anything over a few seconds and his gear becomes an old transport and burn device. It's simpler that way, but there's no point the rest of them following suit; it would only delay proceedings and for what? To even give it consideration would be detrimental to their code-work. They'll leave such shambolic gesturing to the lovers, whose hideous fusings are barely more advanced than their descendents' ridiculous attachments to brain-stem matter and spatio-temporal continuity.

And he returns again to the polished resilience of the fever-struck.

"How is it possible to forget the manner of one's birth? As seeds implanted in unsuspecting mothers, we grew like parasitic worms, womb-weary rampagers greedily consuming our helpless incubators, tearing through their nurturing organs, our piranha thug jaws chomping our way into the world, leaving nothing but a few splintered bones to suckle away the pain of our first breaths. How can love survive being born into isolation, our lungs coated in blood, our teeth draped in the trappings of maternal meat? What affections can grow from this tainted seed? What ugly coding is it that looks to wake in its own dead mother? I hardly bear the thought of it. Our cloistered being provides such sallow, hag-ridden fare that only one born with a taste for ailing flesh would regard it as worthy prey. Hate has a more refined palate…"

●

I know how we got here. I know how once social beings became solitary animals unable to function in direct contact with others. I see the blood-splattered boots clumping down the hallway and up the stairs; I hear the murmuring of a thousand internal voices panicking in silence, getting their last words in, processing the information before the information processes them.

It is not a narrative of decline or of progress, although having the two sides was no small comfort to most. If it is to be viewed as a tale of our ascendance, then it should be compared to the enchanted climb of the cordyceps-infested ant, as alone in the canopy we sit, our bodies little more than roots to a deranging idea still in hibernation. The bony growth will one day erupt through my skin and discharge its poisonous spores aloft with me attached to them; I will ride my way out of here on the back of a toxin puff, each of its spores wearing my smile forever.

21st Century Cunt Factory – built with its doors open – churned out legions of sincere insurgents, those that mutinied against the utility of deception, mutinied against what had made them clever. They herded like stinking, bow-legged cattle and lauded the retard for his glass-skulled honesty – as if he'd overcome the ability to hide it. ("Dare's not an ance a falseness inim. E is what e is." You could be barbequing your neighbours' pets, fucking their toddlers through their soiled nappies and pissing up their front doors, but as long as you weren't trying to hide it – well shit, that's alright then. "The man carn elp what e is. E never tried ta be uver'n what e woz. E woz a right lazy cunt, mind."…)

Logic wasn't their strong point, but luckily for them it was hideously out of fashion, stooped in the inglenook, head bowed, talking to itself, enraptured with neglect, diseased by the shit it ate.

Rat-eyed, thin-lipped parents self-tutored (sometimes there is no decent substitute for proper schooling) in controlled blubbing began killing their children in elaborate ways, ways specifically designed to baffle authorities and garner sympathy for themselves. What a glorious stage while it lasted: endless spin-off deals, 24-hour coverage, newspapers stained with their tearless resolve, their feigned gullibility. The innovators had it easy, but it wasn't long before everyone tired of the spectacle, and then it wasn't about truth or guilt, it was about whether or not they were playing the game. Do we like them? Are they trying to be liked? Can they give us the performance we demand of them? "Not a fucking tear. Who's she trying to kid? Why doesn't she cry for us? Doesn't she care what we think? People like that deserve everything they get; bring it on themselves – no other way to see it."

It was the performance that mattered, and the rules were firmly established: these are the prescribed dramatic equations of grief, sincerity, intelligence, talent, sanity, happiness... The self-loathing of the masses escalated exponentially as the heroes came to resemble the worshippers. Within a few years we had the first wave of drive-by self-abusers: daft, middle-aged housewives fattened on the dream of youth opened their veins on unsuspecting pedestrians, showering them with warm gummy blood and putting the blame on them. Self-styled vagrants popping up everywhere from city centres to the smallest village market place. They emptied their bowels into their trousers, and decorated their faces with the excrement – blacked them up like minstrels, brown and crispy-coated like racist confectionary.

The streets were crowded out with over-realized objects.

Long-decayed sharks flaunted their grey skins to the pinks, and smiled the soil of a thousand half-eaten dinners...

As a boy I saw footage of the now legendary Marvin the Magnificent, who'd attracted little attention at the time, but has since come to be regarded as something of a trailblazer among my select circle. His act was simple but brilliant: he ate himself. His show was called 'Marvin the Marvin Eater', and attracted fairly good ratings to begin with, but before long (a pair of legs and nine fingers down) poor viewing figures meant that his first attempt ended prematurely. A month later he decided to continue, viewers or no viewers. A small network took him up and he set about completing his meal. Despite obvious pressure to get on with it, he took his time: he was a craftsman. He was, however, forced to rush the final stages for two reasons: (1) the ever-present threat of incapacity, and (2) the network threatening to cut him off. His elaborate system of plug-ins meant that his head could be sustained by tubes attached to synthesized organs stored in an adjoining room. This allowed him to consume all but his head, esophagus and stomach (by this point tearing under the strain), pause for a minute or two, and then, with some assistance, tuck into what remained. Inevitably, it all ended up as undigested slop dripping through the back of his ribcage onto the floor. He managed to eat the lips off his face before the show came to an end.

Now there was a parasite that took host-sickness to the next level

●

He has never left his container, and yet, as already evidenced, he's crawling with first-person observations of places he's never been and of scenes he's never been present to witness.

Welcome to the infamous Raj Working Men's Club (Courtesy of memory-transfers from his father, Johnny – The Trap – Logan): stooped men soaked in bile-coloured lighting, cocooned in oak panelled walls and hunting scenes dripping in nicotine, Indian rugs thick with grime that mute the steady percussion of feet, velvet curtains fused with must, ornately corniced ceilings speckled with the fuzz of blowfly, Victorian hardwood bar bathed in alcohol and ruined heads, defunct candelabra hanging from the ceiling like dead spiders; a wethouse for the damned, the strugglers; a refuge for those that had the need: melancholy cyborgs, logicians honing their trade, rancid-minded trannies, breeding experiments, trappers, builders of impossible objects, writers, killers, philosophers... every kind of outmoded depth-seeker huddled together beneath bombinating striplights.

Tommy the Whore-Killer: I jus can't get a break.

Concerned Friend: It's a dead trade, Tom mate; there's no fackin kudos in it no more... A guy I na dug up that English princess, you na the one, screwed her rotten arse, and then projected the footage onta the Palace walls, and the sorry cunt couldn't even make the nationals, so your butchered slags ain't got a chance, old son; don't matter ow many of em you process, it ain't ever gonna be enough.

Tommy the Whore-Killer: But a fowsen of the fackers gotta be worf suink. [Concerned Friend shakes his head slowly, a sympathetic smile rubbing along the sugared edge of his cocktail glass.] But a fowsen... all readily traceable to me... Fack, woz a man to do? Sall facked up.

Ugly George sits in the corner flicking through the glossies with some skinny t-girl. She has the smooth white legs of a porn star, gold lamé hot pants, her rack sunk to the bone under a skin-tight vest, her arms inked up with flattering portraits of herself as a forces pin-up.

"Ow bout this one?" A three-inch cunt-pink fingernail taps at a picture of some child starlet out on the town in Marilyn's white dress.

"Already had her… You're not paying attention. The hardening round the mouth, the 2000-yard stare, the jagged brow lines. Sort it out, yah sorry bean-flicker."

"The three stigmata of Ugly George, well excuse fucking me. And that was a one-off, you know that. Ere's me trying ta elp you out, n all you can do is… Well fuck you…"

"Just maybe I fack you."

"Just try it, darling: You get that thing inside me you'll never get it out: I'll fucking snap it off."

"Dream on, yah slack-arsed cunt."

Sucked into an old routine, they laugh it up before returning to their pile of glossies. "No, but really, George, sometimes you take… Hang on! Who the fuck is this? Now there's no way you've been anywhere near that."

They both sit, crookbacked, making postcards of her future. They are silent. Ugly George starts to drool. His pink-haired apprentice sucks on her fingernails, a look of disquieted pride about her lean face.

"She will do nicely – veeery nicely indeeed."

Ugly George was a celebrity rapist, in both senses: he raped beautiful celebrities and so became something of a celebrity himself. He would only pick out the finest female specimens for his attention: long-legged, exhaustively preened, Amazonian wonders and voluptuous Hollywood babes: pert-breasted, blight-free angels, fresh faces empty of life.

Two trappers sit talking on the dimly-lit mezzanine; a third lays slumped alongside them on a sofa. Papa Johnny is reminiscing:

"I've killed more pelts than I have brains enough to remember. Still remember me first though. He had his head down a toilet in the underpass pisser just off Rathouse Square, and I simply put my gun to the back of his head and blew his face down the pan. Didn't skin him. Shame, fat fuck woulda hung nice in the right apartment. Left him there, his arms and legs scuttling and scratching at the floor like some cat burying its own shit."

"I'm getting myself inside as soon as I get my face back," his fellow trapper interjects. He licks round his piranha mouth with an eel tongue, scratching at the mesh of his fly eyes with a mangled two-fingered stump.

"I ain't about to hide away like the others – not yet. I get the fidgets so bad I can hear my muscles talk; it's like they're trying to uproot themselves from my bones. I don't have the funds to go inside anyhow, so outside's the only place to be. And you get to like them walls you ain't ever coming back."

(A Jellyfish can never come out of its box once it has turned. If forced out, those lucent bubbles of venal snot are torn apart in seconds. They were the first of the lock-downs: people choosing to go in, cutting themselves off from others almost entirely. It was them that led the way for The Seclusion Programme.)

Johnny lived out with the animals that knew they were lost: they saw their own abhorrence reflected in the faces around them. He lived amongst the whores, the breeding-experiments, the gecko-eyed pinballers with faces like lizard-skin gasmasks, the dealers, the pornographers and the pimps, the waste of a city that had gone into hibernation. He lived amongst those he killed, in order to procure a future he had no desire to live out. He skinned men and women for those inside who paid for their hides (which they then hung on their walls), and who paid to be inside his head as he did it – all the fun of the kill and none of the risk. Sometimes he'd kill them before he skinned them and sometimes he wouldn't.

His home was one of universal rot and malfunction: rust-munched automobiles, cobwebs the size of shark-nets, untended gardens merging into one another; patches of thorn-blown wilderness creeping ever closer together, their towering buddleia eating into the perpetually low, late-summer sun, aimless trails of silver slug gunk criss-crossing the city, the accumulated crap of delirious spending sprees spilling out onto the pavements, ornamental, useless.

His arms and legs were encased in metal. He had the head of a Rottweiler. He wore black leather gloves, and a grey and black uniform from the time when his murderous practices had another name, back when the war was around to keep them all company. He had a dog's head on his shoulders for the same reason that other men had the heads of panthers, orang-utans, hyenas, goats, mutant conger eels, toads, preying mantises... They had these heads because they were once fighting men, because they are dehumanising, because their brains were elsewhere, along with their faces, under lock and key, and nobody saw the need to give them back when the war ended. Their new heads were full of transmitters, remotely connected to their brains and a (supposedly) crumbling central mainframe controlled by what was left of army intelligence. Johnny, unlike some of his cyborg brethren, had resisted destroying his transmitters in order to free himself from control. He'd seen what happens when connections are destroyed, seen them left on the fringes of personhood, prey to a bottomless reservoir of the basest urges.

The war took its toll: a black yolk sunrise threw its dirty rays over the city like an old grey prison blanket, and weary soldiers emptied the fumes of war from their lungs.

The third trapper – head of a wasp, all twitching antennae and saliva-soaked mandibles – takes a needle from his moonscape eye and slumps back into the imploded sofa. His legs shift to and fro, conducting the hit of wakeful death throughout his limp body as he spies a squad car pull up outside. He puts his hand on his gun and yawns, his wet black jaws clenching like some restorative vaginal exercise.

All patrons of the Raj had reason to fear the squads, but the trappers, perhaps, had more to fear than most. Their murderous enterprises were unsanctioned, and by selling off access to their consciousnesses they had severely impaired the quality of the data that fed back into the mainframe. Once a squad got hold of a trapper, his hunting days were through.

At the bar, a couple of impossible-construction workers bemoan their trade:

"The work gets ta me. The fings I see. Takes me free o these jus ta convince me me arms n legs are anyfing ta do wi me. Can't sleep for shit either."

"I hear yah. Still, sgood to ave some work for a change. I na it's only dismantlin', but it beats dismantlin yerself."

"Yah reckon?"

"'Nother one?"

"Why not. Do for the orrors if nuffin else."

The impossible roller coasters now stand abandoned, their shifting tracks screwing with the eyes and upstaging the brain. You'll rarely see an animal within 50 metres of one, and if you do the laxative effect is brutal: their rectums go into spasm, draining the bowel of its contents before draining the dog of the bowel. They never rust; they repel even the breeze. But it's an old trick now, a stale ride, with no repeat fares: a good way to lose your kids for a... a good way to lose your kids. They were quite the thing for a while, attracting not only the attention of the thrill-seekers and candy-floss brigade, but also those not ordinarily

associated with fairground rides: religious types, undercover ge-
ometers, mathematicians, physicists, Escher enthusiasts, etc. It
was a head-fuck for all that had a head worth fucking. Nobody
came back for more; one go was always enough and often too
much, especially if you were unfortunate enough to get the bars
down in a faulty car, and go slip outside the operational sphere
of the custom-made PLCs (Programmable Logic Controllers).
Those poor bastards got their money's worth alright: their rides
went on indefinitely; some had to wait for the deconstruction
teams to find them, by which time they had invariably come un-
done, and some were never found.

A Logic Squad is on the doorstep.

The lights flicker to warn the members. Logic Squads
(some of which are now free-roaming Paradoxites) were created
to clamp down on unsanctioned theoretics. Anyone aspiring to
divulge meaning beyond the bland physicality of their being was
incarcerated, publicly ridiculed and disposed of as an enemy of
human flourishing. It was the duty of the masses to enjoy themselves, to take the prescribed drugs, to take an interest in each
other, and leave the big theory ("There are no gaps; trust us.")
to those qualified to make the best of it. It was not advisable for
anyone else to concern themselves with meaning or truth; utility would only suffer, and for what? ("What sane person could
have a problem with being happy? Who would actively seek out
misery and failure? Such irrational behaviour cannot be permitted. For their own sake and the sake of those around them they

must be helped. If making people happy is a crime, then we are proud to be criminals.")

Felicity Inc. began its series of Pleasure Policies with an Arts Programme; it saturated the scene with undercover agents posing as writers, artists, film-makers, etc. These agents practiced the old arts only in order to popularize and debase them: marketing men sucking the sense out of art and literature by dressing it up as entertainment, feeding it to a mass audience, killing it with hollow merchandise and over-exposure – masterpieces synopsized to death. ("Look at this crybaby bullshit peddled by archaic artisans bobbing in their own tears, hoping to drown everyone else before they go under. See how awful it is, how anti-life it is. Life at all costs! Life at all costs!") Any creations deemed not to be life-affirming were destroyed, the creators 'educated'. The new society needed to take pleasure in itself; its members had to look at each other: they were the work now. To separate the art object from the artist was to deny the wonder of humanity for the sake of the artifacts it could produce. The tawdry trinkets of the old creators only served to distract us from the true spectacle: the creator himself. Most people made their tongues ache lapping themselves up. Everyone wanted to be told that they were interesting, that they were worth other people's attention and that others like them were worth theirs.

Those that frequented the Raj – and other like-minded establishments that brewed their own booze, refusing to sell the state-licensed Cheer Beer and High Spirits – didn't buy it. They saw the game even if most of them didn't see the underlying objective. They'd seen too much of life to think of happiness as anything but a shackle on the truth. What they didn't see was that they were just as integral to the mechanics of the game as the moon-faced morons with numbers on their backs: the goal nets were stitched from their dissent.

Black, warm, soft-walled cell telling me it's time to leave... Birthing-teeth through the cord like a mole rat... My first taste of blood... Twitching, embryonic eyes looking for light... Gagging on the world... Chewing, chewing, chewing through my homeland into the striplight sun... Fetal gill-slits flooded with blood... Lost, tunneling through fat and unborn shit... The sky screams somewhere in the distance... Soft skull knocking on bone... Tiny arms pushing and tearing, paddling a course... Feet caught in intestinal snares... Into hidden skin, elastic glasshouse... Lips screwed back into my face... Purple light and blood-free air... The sky screams somewhere in the distance... Closer, fading away... Baby snarls... A feast of animal love on the slaughterhouse floor... Head prize-bobbing in the slop... Her face... Her face has left its mass behind... The mucoid privilege of her dead eyes... My heart screams somewhere in the distance...

Dreams of Amputation

All the tools of his pending peregrination streaming across the screens in front of him, world-code slipping away with every fresh page. His nerves are noisy with the wait, the fear of uncertain expectancy. How long before it senses something is awry, before it blindsights their scheme and takes steps to prevent any abrasion to its mass? If it breaks their code it'll shut them down in seconds. It'll scramble the amputation dream into a precaution-script for its own use, a down-time warning device, should there be any followers willing to risk dissolution. ZS1's tomb-speak operation has kept it at bay so far – with the occasional glitch seared off at connection – and now he's soaring, replete with the abstract diseases that will suck their skins dry.

Papa Johnny eventually came in by way of one of his best customers. Food was drying up on the outside: the delivery vehicles were becoming increasingly hard to penetrate, and the taste of rat-fed quasi-human meat was an uninspiring reward for the effort it took to procure. As time went on the only life left out on the streets came in the shape of neoplastic whores, their minds fucked into crumpled submission, old soldiers dead-headed from the mainframe, surviving on a diet of vermin and dirt, the first wave of Spectre-Mules, and a few stubborn Trappers tirelessly picking off the remaining skins before they forced themselves to make a choice. The Outsiders had slowly killed themselves off; the faceless carrion, replaced in breeding rooms, went unmourned by their unseen leader. But Johnny knew how to survive; his existence was founded on the deaths of those around him – a point of logic, no less – and was intent that it remain so.

Hamilton Jones IX had been using the services of one Johnny 'Dog-Head' Logan for close to a decade, and had over that time developed quite a habit. He dreaded the complete collapse of the outside world, but was resigned to its inevitability nonetheless. He knew he couldn't keep hold of Johnny for much longer, but the thought of one more project kept him going. "Call it the eccentricity of a gentleman if you will, old boy, but I shall sorely miss you when all this comes to an end," was his standard refrain on the matter, and pomposity aside he meant every word.

The only child of a well-respected property tycoon, Hamilton Jones IX wanted for nothing but character. Despite residing in one of the city's premiere dwellings, with assets beyond his comprehension, his only real pleasure came courtesy of Johnny's willingness to sell murder. Hamilton had no real intellect, and his powers of concentration were weaker than the muscles in his lazy eye, which he disguised by taping up the relevant lens of his black-rimmed spectacles. His schoolboy appearance was further enhanced by his black hair, which was cropped short around the sides and at the back, almost to the skin, but left long on top, parted down the middle like a na-ïve seabird. He regularly quoted Shakespeare, and threw Latin tags into conversation whenever he could, especially when talking with types that he felt sure he'd impress without question – Johnny, ever respectful when it came to his customers, was one such type. But the respect he showed his gaggle of gutless turds was entirely utilitarian; he despised them all, and on many occasions would have liked nothing more than to see his blade swimming through their muscle.

Johnny made Hamilton Jones IX his last call. He knew he'd be the one to miss him the most, and so delayed passing on news of his retirement to the last minute.

"Do come up, old bean." He is excited at the prospect of a new project, cock twitching in his pants like a crone's finger.

Johnny enters the lift and waits for the door to shut. Within a few seconds it is 50 floors up and he is stepping out into the conversation room. The room, though large, has no furniture and no other doors. The only feature is a large window that allows you to look into another exactly similar room. Johnny walks over to the window for the last time. His customer is sat on a white leather chair, his knees locked together like a prissy schoolgirl. "Alright Hamilton, ows fings?"

"Just great, old boy, just great, now you're here, just great. Now do tell me what we're discussing today. What's the topic? Are we ready for another? I do hope so. Come, come, mox nox in rem."

"Sorry but it's bad news. Givin the game up. Nowt but rats n corpses out there anyhow."

"Oh well, olim meminisse iuvabit. But no... surely... There simply must be something we can do. They can't all be gone."

"They ain't, but I will be, as from today."

"You're giving up on me? You're giving up on me; that's it isn't it. O Villainy, villainy! Is there no way? Surely we can squeeze in just one more. I can't be left like this, not like this. What say you?"

"I register in a cappla ours. I'll be a jellyfish like you wivin a week."

"But you'll go to one of those frightful boxes. They're little more than veal crates, old boy; I won't have it; that's no life for a man like you."

"A man like me ain't got much choice."

"It is unmanly grief, I know. But I find this ending too abrupt to bear with any dignity. And aren't there always choices?"

"Not that I can see. The outside's over: sall bots n vermin. Nowt else for me to do." Johnny turns to leave.

Up on his feet, all composure lost, Hamilton Jones IX shouts after him: "I can think of one."

Johnny turns round. "What?"

"Me... We'll skin me. It'll be magnificent: I'll plug into you as always, and then we can do me. And once we've finished you can have this place. What say you, old chap? One last project?"

"I get to stay here?"

"Of course. Of course. I wouldn't have it any other way. Do we have a deal?"

He had a deal.

When Johnny realized that Hamilton was for real he could barely keep his tongue behind his teeth. He was treated to a guided tour of his new home, and a lengthy dissection of the implications of detached self-murder before finally they embarked upon their culmination.

The last (borrowed) words of Hamilton Jones IX:

"Dead life, blind sight, poor mortal living ghost,

Woe's scene, world's shame, grave's due by life usurped,

Brief abstract and record of tedious days,

Rest thy unrest on England's lawful earth,

Unlawfully made drunk with innocent blood!

[A pause to drain the last drop of anticipation from failing life. Half lamb, half wolf, he hollers out his closing line, half dead, half alive… half…]

Then kill, kill, kill, kill, kill, kill!"

Johnny gave him the full treatment, as far as that was possible. He worked the blade slow, took it under and pared his muscle meticulously, just the way Ham liked it. Unfortunately, if not surprisingly, there was little resistance from the victim – nothing but the odd jerk of involuntary self-preservation for Ham to get worked up about. But Johnny felt sure he'd made up for this absence with attention lavished elsewhere: a flawless decortication of the skull, a crazed savaging of thigh muscle, and a number of exquisitely staggered dismemberments to name but a few.

Johnny assumed Ham's existence with ease. Nobody ever came calling. Nobody had a need to. He became a watcher, shunning the broadcast option for obvious reasons, and nobody suspected a thing, or if they did, didn't consider it worth their effort to rectify. He planned to live out his days in there: within 10 years he'd be a 30-stone retard hooked on the screen and the lives of a thousand different fuckwits the world over. (Over-indulgence on this scale and the resultant stress on the Spectre-Mules were two of the strongest arguments put forward for the introduction of 100% food supplementation.)

One of the first things he sought out when he took possession of Hamilton's place was the hermetically sealed door leading down into the underground walkway, and since then he'd spent hours just looking at it, placing his hands on its metal tegument and imagining himself down there with normal people, eating, drinking, shopping, and riding the escalators up outside into the Safe Zones for more of the same, for a life that he distantly remembered being not only desirable but rightfully his.

Johnny never found the courage to open the door, preferring instead to have its possibilities remain unsullied by experience.

Dreams of Amputation

The dump-tube light is still flashing. He reaches over and retrieves its contents. They hold no surprise, little does: a small packet of body-inhibitors to give him a taste. He sits down and gets them straight down his neck. In a couple of minutes his cerebellum will be fighting for its life, a fight it is destined to lose all the while its adversary is in his system. He makes some last minute checks while he's still able to move.

The abrupt frustration of movement never fails to catch him off guard; it is as if the drug stalks the portended presence of that one instant when he will momentarily relax into himself, and pounces immediately it appears. The truth, of course, is that his expectation was never up to the task: the drug kicks in when it kicks in, and that it always seems to him as though he'd been primed for it right up until that point is a delusion, for he never has been and never could be. There is a definite trace of fear as his body recedes and his eyesight dims: the final, vain striving of defeated anatomy.

He sits, calmly awaiting some pithy stab of disquiet.

He runs through the drill, telling himself the conditions under which he is forced to exist, reminding himself of just what a filthy burden his body is, unmarking the self for flight.

In due course, as the body pressures his dislocated self to become reacquainted, he prepares himself for a miserable return.

He gets up from his work station, ZS1's words still falling down his screens, a raven downpour on lighted window panes. Takes a distracted stroll round his tiresomely familiar home. He makes wide, anti-clockwise circuits of the central pillar, feeling the faultless surface of the walls with flat palms, his hands ever-empty of change. He passes his rest area, its gleaming white mattress defying any signs of use. He completes his compass and keeps going, all the while consciously connecting his movements to the unfilled metallic resonance of footfalls.

After passing the last of the screens on his ninth circuit he feels a discrepancy in the flooring, a distinct instability beneath his left foot. He crash-lands into a forgotten fleshiness, the mere thought of there being a flaw in his container's design making roots in the resultant terror, fixing him to the spot. He gets down on his knees.

One of the floor panels is loose. He pushes down on its four corners repeatedly, disbelieving the rocking motion, the rattling, wishing it away. The trickery of revisited tissue; what else can it be?

He walks away from the floor panel, hoping that when he returns its position will have altered. On finding the situation unchanged, he decides to challenge this supposed flaw head-on by wrenching the panel from its housing. He finds a suitable lever and jams it under the raised corner. The panel slips up out of the ground to reveal a brightly lit, metal-lined hole descending some 10 metres. There is a ladder up one side and what looks like a tunnel at the bottom.

This is hard for him to take. He's been in there too long for surprises to be possible; it's like him finding another nose on his face. He has to avert his eyes. He retches, tasting the lie of undigested food at the back of his throat. He turns round and looks over at the screens in an attempt to foster his brain to their calming spill. He stares at the symbols, momentarily losing himself in the tireless jostling.

If you want to see what it is we ran from, look to when the search for meaning became its own goal, and then look beyond at what was found. Look at the ancient traveller's wide eyes. Listen to the smug purring of that intrepid failure. Look at how the search is passed down like some faecal heirloom: ("Put it somewhere safe, somewhere you can't see or smell it! Make yourself another one for everyday use, and make sure you construct it out of the best materials you can find! How will you know... uh... well just find something you like the look of...") If you want to understand the tools of despair, look at the little men that work them but never get to see what it is they are building, and never care enough to ask. But if you want to see something to really put a ghoul in your guts then go back and dine with a humanist, watch the blood of brutalized children pour from the edges of his blistered mouth. Watch his eyes fill up with infected tears, voice parroting exotic shrieks of rape, disfigurement and death from too many unseen distant lands. And if you can hold onto the contents of your stomach for long enough, stick around for the brainless twine he uses to knot his crusade.

He decides to enter the shaft and see where it leads. Knowing it will not be possible to ignore its presence, he can think of no other alternative.

As he makes the descent he can feel the pinch of exertion in his arms and legs. His limbs are thin, with very little muscle tone, and negotiating himself down the ladder is a slow and arduous affair. Once at the bottom he has another decision to make: which direction to follow the tunnel? Concluding that he'll eventually have to investigate both directions, he chooses to go left from the ladder without further deliberation. The lights are triggered by motion sensors, so at no point can he see much beyond the space he's occupying. His initial steps are tentative.

The cylindrical tunnel has a diameter of not much more than a metre, so he is forced to either stoop right over, with his hands on his knees to retain balance, or crawl. He ends up alternating between the two: one minute shuffling like a lame dog, the next staggering about like some starveling sumo wrestler. His progress is impeded further by his physical weakness and the rapid onset of lumbar pains.

Eventually he comes upon the bottom of a ladder. Despite being wary of what might be at the other end of it, he is relieved to have encountered something, anything. He straightens up in the vertical shaft and immediately begins pulling himself up the ladder. He can see the domed roof of a container above him as he climbs; he hears nothing but the sounds of his clattering ascendance.

He crawls out of the hole onto the floor. The container is indistinguishable from his own. He looks for differences, but finds none. It is a perfect replica. Even the screens are streaming the escapee's code.

A far as he can remember he's never met another person. Not one he could actually touch. (Flashes of a dead mother.) And his memory goes all the way back. (But there's a gap he can't taste. Reborn at nearly a year.) But this life-long isolation isn't exactly a rarity, the difference here being that he has managed to inhabit the memories of men who have met and touched others – touched them to death in Johnny's case. He sees how fucked up all this would seem to them. The lives led now were the reserve of jailed demons, and even they had their screws to abuse. Even memories of massacres manage to spark a feeling of nostalgia some-where inside him, nostalgia for the stark intimacy of ridding something of its life. He's as bad as Johnny's clients when it comes down to it.

He knows of human emotions. He understands their workings. He has knowledge of them somehow, and yet he's largely free of any resultant interference. He knows that many of them are born from insipidness and idiotic passions, and he believes there's supposed to be a 'but', but he doesn't see the need for one. He is also aware that because he doesn't feel the emotions he claims to know, that it is questionable whether he really knows them, but that's up for debate. When he experiences what he takes to be the symptoms of, for example, fear or loneliness he must admit to feeling detached from the emotions, as if he is recognizing them in someone else. There are few things about which this is not true.

"It is in those few things that you truly reside."

He hears the voice and knows it to be spurious, but still he hears the voice. Why can he not be rid of it? What use is it to him? Just another gap he'll have to fill before his future comes.

He remembers the philosophers dead with detail, and how they honed their trade into the grave for the sake of their livelihoods. Incapable of audacity, they pleasured themselves with a maze constructed from nothing but dead-ends. They were so petrified that they might happen upon the truth, might come to know something for certain, that they deployed some of their best minds to obliterate it, scattering its shards into infinity. But they were only trying to keep the dream alive, after all, fighting to keep the questions outnumbering the answers, picking away at the odd dropped stitch in an otherwise ever-tightening blanket of sacrosanct precision. They fought hard, if unwittingly, against the encroaching dullness of complete knowledge, but ultimately paid the price of becoming as dull as their enemy – at least the chemical truths of literature sometimes bothered to wear a suit and tie.

The floor panel leaning against the wall in the exact same position seals it: the tunnel is circular. He has ruined himself just to end up where he started – a poisoned allegory of life if ever there was one. Yet despite the conclusiveness of the evidence, he finds himself less than satisfied with the conclusion. After all, it is not impossible that the tunnel is, as it seemed, straight, and this container merely qualitatively identical to his own, which was still there positioned some half-hour to the right.

He wheels the chair over to the rest area, and leans the floor panel up against the central pillar. These changes in place, he climbs back down into the shaft. At the bottom of the ladder he turns to the left, assumes a semi-crouch position, and slowly lures the light back down into the tunnel.

Agent Nolan's office might not be palatial, but it does at least have walls and a door he can shut. That said, in many ways the segregation from the rest of the desks on his floor is merely symbolic, for the walls are so thin that he can hear the mesh of voices just as clearly as if he was sitting in the middle of it. His tiny enclosure does, though, offer the opportunity for him to turn his head in any direction and see objects that remain in place, to see stillness: for a few moments in his working day he is able to allay the motion sickness he gets from the never-ending flurry of purposeful bodies.

On his desk sits a cheap onyx picture frame. Inside it, looking out, hair scattered in the breeze, is Jenny.

Nolan leans forward and traces a line around her face with his right index finger, ignoring the fingers on his left hand that slowly embed themselves into the worn upholstery of his chair. The display panels, out of which his face is constructed, conveyed a wink and a used-up smile – all the warmth of a frazzled porn-star. (Nolan is ex-army, but rather than wait forever to retrieve his old head, which most likely had ceased to exist anyway, it having been reconstituted along with thousands of others in some skin farm, he'd had an acquaintance construct him a new one in return for certain leniencies.)

The overall appearance of the face is effective, despite the crudity of finish about the chin and right temple: it consists of a collage of video screens, differing in size and shape, onto which his new face is displayed. Messages from his brain – returned to him, but still indentured to the pool by way of two-way neural transmitters – are translated into an array of pictorial gestures.

He'd chosen the best-looking features on offer, strong, rugged, yet somehow ill-matched, giving him the look of a distinctly Photofit handsomeness. Little effort had been made with the rest of the head, which wears its circuitry like bulging brain tissue, its metal plates like loosely patchworked bone, its wiring like multicoloured veins. The same disregard for finish is present in his mechanical left arm: dull silver spheroids and rods spin and contract for all to see. Originally it had been covered – pink-skin tone and all the features – but he'd not bothered with a replacement after some gator-jawed pinballer chewed through it. He wears white shirts, the sleeves invariably rolled up to his elbows, a black tie loose on the neck, charcoal grey trousers and pointed black slip-ons; on occasion a cigarette dangles from the side of his mouth, churning fake white smoke into his rendered eyes.

On hearing someone at the door he jolts back in his seat as if the picture has dispensed an electrical charge.

"Yes! What is it?" he says.

The door opens and Squad Leader Grice walks in.

"Sit down," says Nolan, pushing a chair out the other end of the desk with his foot.

"I'm not stopping. I came to give you these." Grice pulls a set of keys from his pocket and slides them across the desk. "I won't be needing them for a while. You take them. And see that you use them this time."

"Maybe," says Nolan, flicking his eyes over to Jenny halted in the snow, "maybe I will."

"I won't need them back for a least a month."

"You're staying on in the city?"

"Yes, at my sister's place."

"The place growing on you is it? You usually can't wait to get back to your precious slice of river."

"She's not right. I'm worried about her. Been getting worse for weeks now."

"She still has the flu?"

"It isn't the flu. We thought it was. The doctor said that's what it was. Maybe it was, to begin with. But it's more than that now. You remember how fanatical she was about cooking."

"Cooking and eating, if I remember."

"She barely eats at all now. There's no pleasure in it for her. Her clothes don't fit her anymore."

"You have to force her to eat?"

"No. She eats every day: just enough to stop herself starving."

"Can't say I have much more than that myself."

"I know, but it's the change; it's drastic. She's suddenly obsessed with the comings and goings in her building, and more recently the other buildings in her complex. She makes lists and charts, documenting and collating every detail she can access. I don't like to say – she's my sister – but she's acting like a fucking nutcase."

"I only met her a few times, but she never struck me as the community-spirited type."

"She wasn't; far from it: it was as much as she could do to engage in everyday pleasantries."

"So what now?"

"I'm not sure, but I can't leave her on her own."

"What does the doctor say?"

"He tells me it's not uncommon."

"Nor's death."

"Right! As if that makes it okay. He keeps telling me that he gets a dozen or so fresh cases of sudden OCD in his surgery every week, with nearly all of them displaying the same calculated focus."

"And he prescribes wait-and-see to each and every one of them, I suppose."

"Because the condition isn't life threatening, and the sufferers appear to be content in their condition, they are not considered a priority."

His sympathy pretty much exhausted, Nolan just shakes his head, and opens one of his desk drawers, looking for nothing in particular.

"So you'll go?" asks Grice.

"I'll ask Jenny."

"They'll give her the time off?"

"She's more than due it," says Nolan, struggling to control the panels at the outskirts of his mouth.

"You have to watch those bastards at the Spectre Project: the hours creep up and before you know it there's not much time for anything else. Carlson's wife was doing fourteen-hour days when she fell in front of that train. He reckons his home-life is much the same as it ever was. Then, of course, there was…"

"Jenny's going to cut back on her hours."

"Glad to hear it." He looks at the wall to his right, where there'd once been a clock. "Okay, I'll be going." At the door he turns and says, "If you find you like it, now's the time to buy: lots of people selling up. I don't understand it; given the choice, I'd never leave."

Nolan glances up at him, nods his head and returns to the tranquillity of his still drawer.

Grice closes the door behind him and returns to his desk through a swirl of industrious voices.

It was a month before Johnny happened upon Hamilton's harem. There were twenty concubines in all, eighteen alive and two dead (one, a Necro800, was designed dead; the other had died when the batteries in her vibrating pussy had leaked, poisoning her blood); it was quite a collection. Ham had failed to disclose them during his guided tour, and it was quite by chance that Johnny found their quarters: a gargantuan dome situated on the top of his building above the roof-terrace canopy.

The whole place hummed with frustrated purpose.

Dreams of Amputation

An eight-year old girl was sitting on the floor in front of
him as he entered. She had the mind and the voice box of an
eighty-year old paedophile who was staring down between her
legs watching the frantic movements of her skinny little fingers.
(Sales Pitch: "Have your fun and take revenge on a filthy per-
vert in the process. Make his arse bleed and don't even let him
watch.") In the distance he saw the polished calves of a 25-foot
Amazon, muscles wrenched into shape by a pair of high-heels
patterned to resemble a New York skyline. Passing close by,
he got the chills from a gilt-edged vitrine housing Hamilton's
Necro800; the very picture of death-sex, maintained at whatever
stage of decomposition you desire, she provides the ultimate experience for the sexual necrotroph.

A transsexual horse/human hybrid clip-clopped up to him,
amber flanks glistening under the spotlights. Johnny looked her
up and down: thoroughbred racer's hind quarters, tail swishing,
human cock hanging between them like a gnarly piece of rope,
smooth, white-skinned torso, substantial rack, slender neck
topped off with a huge fucking horse head. It was quite a sight
even for Logan.

They began closing in on him.

A CashmereDP50 (an old-school classic) smiled and
preened her fur. Through her Lycra knickers Johnny could see
the built-in cock banging away at her, hear the loose sacks slap-
ping against her anus; judging by the vigorous shifting of her
gusset, it must have been cranked right up to its ferocity setting.

She paid it no attention whatsoever, as if each stroke was little more than a second heartbeat. Two passive abuse models joined the throng hand in hand. You could beat the living shit out of these genuflecting beauties, put bullets through their brains, slice them from cunt to chin, decorate them with their innards, but as long as you remembered to place them back in their capsules in good time, they'd be as good as new and ready for more within the hour. Our Hamilton Jones IX had felt insecure about using the aggression upgrades, and they remained uninstalled.

"Hello. My name is Lucinda, and yours?" The horse head has the tongue of English royalty – plummy, vacant.

"Johnny… Johnny – The Trap – Logan, Johnny Dog-head Logan… Johnny'll do."

"Such picaresque variations. Just great. I love them: so very roguish. You must be quite the thing, Mr. Johnny – The Trap – Logan. But before I lose my thread I simply must enquire as to the whereabouts of our Hammy."

"E's dead, and Johnny'll do."

"DEAD!" The word does a circuit, deftly leaping from mouth to mouth. There is even a resounding knock on the glass from the Necro800, not wishing to be left out of proceedings, especially as she, more than any of them, knows the true nature of his loss.

"'Fraid so, a month back. I bin ere ever since. E never said nuffin bout you lot, though. Guess you were his dirty little secret. Nah offence like."

"None taken, Mr. Johnny – The…, Johnny. We are each of us dirty in our own way, and quite secret. Although many of us, as you can see, are far from little." She strokes her cock all the way to its tip, and whinnies in satisfaction.

"Not my thing, darlin – Ham I ain't."

"I can see that, Johnny, but what will become of us?"

Johnny allowed them to stay – well most of them. Some had to leave. The Black Widow was the first to go: the 8 spindly legs erupting from her ribcage gave him the terrors, and her twat, covered in hundreds of tiny red eyes, was a sight he wasn't willing to risk repeating. He couldn't even have her in the same building, so he threw her off the roof. He even made sure of her mangled corpse, in case she had managed to cling to the wall at some point during her descent. She was busted up good and proper: through his telescope she looked like a black star at sundown. The Skinless Wonder went the same way. The sight of her patchwork tissues flexing, twisting and bubbling like a suit of snakes was a sickness that he wasn't prepared to buy into.

It takes him twice as long to reach the second ladder, (or, as the facts seem to imply, to come upon the same ladder for a second time). He'd had to stop a few times to prevent his joints seizing up. As he struggles upward rung by rung he recognizes dread, unmistakable dread. He concentrates on the sensations, pushing it right back into his body, refusing to translate it into psychology.

He crawls out onto the floor like some forlorn insect. He senses immediately that this isn't his container. The thought was there last time, but now it is strong, too strong to ignore. The chair is where he moved it, as is the floor panel, but these facts seem to hold no consequence. The lie has make-up.

He gets to his feet and goes over to the screens. He studies the rainfall.

The central screen goes blank. No more than two seconds later a picture emerges, a picture of him in his container standing where he is standing looking at the central screen, confusion scratched into his face giving it the appearance of a mask. They stand looking at each other. He raises his hand; he raises his hand on screen. He tips his head from side to side; he tips his head from side to side on screen. And yet he knows this is no mirror, for he is not there. They share many things, but not all things. He is so confident that he does not even flinch when he sees an Airworm cloud hovering above his screen head. Not even a tickle of alliance does he feel as they divide into two thin streams and pour into his ears.

The screen face begins to quail.

His is serene.

The arms and legs buck his screen body into formless jelly.

His remain still.

An exit wound leaks his liquidized interior onto the metal floor.

His skin harbours no such mutilation.

His infiltrators fly free from his empty cutis and it drops to the ground.

He stands in front of the screens, organs intact, body still riddled with a life undeniably his.

Did nobody wonder what would happen when audience became act, when watched became everything and watching nothing? Small Stranger was born and nobody could forgo the attention for fear of crumbling into a pile of lonely unattended scraps. The internal eye, neglected and debased for decades, shrivelled like a spent gland, the bogus selves it had helped to invent now resurgent in the lacquered eyes of performing drones. This was the time of the spectral awakenings: enforced, arbitrary downgrades manufacturing a sub-population of ravenous voyeurs – out there, voiceless consumers of image, word and sound. And so the reconstruction of externalized selves began under the ever-watching eyes of these man-made Berkeleyan gods, the Spectre8s. (Cross-wired solipsists of the world unite to thank their prefab audience and their ruptured brain tissue – at least they would if they could spare the time.)

The Spectre8 is a pathetic sight. Its overworked eyes and press-ganged brain have a way of distorting the appearance of its head: it appears to flicker before your eyes, as if what you see on those knitted shoulders is nothing more than a projected image, some flick-book delusion. All 137 million eyes within eyes, each with its own nerve-line to the pink porridge sucking in its screens, vistas of artificial depth hypnotizing their prey and tunneling into their butchered brains. Nobody can afford to sneer at this enlightened reciprocity, this fractal jewel of Platonic justice; nobody can afford to be offended by the Spectre8s' grey/blue skin and guttering manifestation, their crumpled skeletons, tapping fingers and atrophied muscles; and nobody can undermine the value of the prancers' theatre, their endless self-referencing and splayed ribcages, their lunatic over-farmed consciousnesses. The loop is protected both inside and out by the hazard-clasp of identity; it's in nobody's interests to disrupt this cycle, and so it remains and so it shall remain.

Aside from a few details, it's a standard Spectre8 cubicle: 27 screens (one large central screen surrounded by a web of 26 smaller screens), low blue-tinged lighting, a fully operational maintenance unit located on the back wall, a black ergonomic recliner positioned at the optimum distance of 172cm from the media panel, and a flip-over keyboard secured over the occupant's lap. Being that 68% of all Spectre8s are female, it comes as no surprise that the occupant in this particular instance helps to make up that percentage.

Dreams of Amputation

She has many of the trademark features: the appearance of material instability from the neck up, her blue face shimmering like an ersatz river, eyes occupied and lost, fingertips capped in protective sheaths... But you can only go so far with the similarities, for this cubicle boasts a number of deviations worthy of mention.

Standing alongside her, just outside her peripheral vision, is a three-legged walnut table and a leather armchair. Placed on top of the table is a crystal vase belching out a dozen wild roses from its splayed neck. Spectre8s are unable to appreciate anything but the media panel, making any such decoration completely pointless. There's also her arse-length blonde hair to be taken into account, combed down her body in two panels like some shiny waistcoat, when all other Spectre8s are completely bald, the roots of any hair follicles having been zapped. In addition to these oddities, she isn't plumbed into her chair, suggesting that she is being supplied with HB pills, which is something of an unnecessary extravagance for someone in her condition.

Oh, and she has a name, Jennifer Sprill, a name that someone still uses to address her, a name of significance for that someone – a name that signifies absence more than it does presence.

A red light comes on above the door. Moments later the door opens. She is oblivious to the visitor's presence. She remains securely anchored to her screens. Nolan comes and sits beside her in the leather armchair. He appears restless, rearranging the flowers, and gently smoothing down the ends of her hair.

"Hey, Jen, not long now. Things are finally coming together. Won't be too long now…"

He stands up, takes a few steps back and surveys the cubicle. He can sense alterations, but no matter where he looks he cannot pinpoint what or where they might be. He can see that everything is in place, but still he continues to look for discrepancies, unable to shake the feeling that something, some subtle modification, is eluding him. It's as if certain of the cubicle's contents, Jenny included, have been moved and then returned to their rightful place. There's a forced deliberateness about their arrangement. The placement is perfect and yet he cannot shake the feeling that the order is merely mimicking the one he left behind after his last visit.

"Anything you want to tell me, Jen?"

He sits back down and begins inspecting her at close quarters, bringing her hands right up to his eyes, almost burying his head into the fabric of her dress. He scours her meticulously for more than half an hour before proceeding with his duties. Despite finding nothing out of place, the usual sense of easy belonging he associates with that cubicle remains indelibly fractured.

He feels his body cajoling him into a retroactive slink. He does not succumb. He's past all that now. He remains calm. He remains.

"I am my body's infestation. I am purity. I am god of emptiness. I am the collective source around which my corrupted pictures swirl in endless coiling turns…"

(He recalled that toward the end of his life his father had claimed that the most frightening thing about death and life was that he had nothing new to say about them. He was rotten with oldness, crippled with truth. But he failed himself this way. He saw only what the void took away, what it lacked; the adjectival austerity overwhelmed its adverbial awe, and he despaired the ruination of what was nothing but needless clutter.)

He retrieves the chair from the rest area and sits down, muscle-burn and raw knees sourcing the past. The screens resume their running of the script. He has to return. He cannot explain to himself why he has to retrace his steps, why there is any less substantial than where he's heading, or why it is that spatial location can have any hold over him whatsoever. He just can't help feeling that there is significance in this contradiction, that there is something to be learned by rewinding his subterranean transit.

Cashmere's entire body was covered in a thin but unbroken layer of androgenic hair. When she spoke it was with a deal of effort: sentences would invariably die half-born on her tongue. Johnny told her she could stay if she put some clothes on and kept out of sight: a double insurance. Her fellow wives agreed for her and whisked her away.

Johnny developed quite a taste for fucking. He'd never had much time for it on the outside. You stuck your dick in anything out there after The Hunger hit and you were never sure to get it back in one piece. He'd heard tales and seen the results of Fly-Trap Tarts who hocked their meat-eating pussies to unsuspecting Johns, locking the poor fuckers in suffocating embraces till such time as their once stiff members had been liquidized and siphoned up into the whore's shrunken gut. Their scale-skinned pimps would finally snap the arms open, and as the fallen lovers fumbled with their bloody stumps he'd put it on them for settlement.

"Pay up, cunt, else you fuck her widya tongue."

"But…"

"No fuckin' 'buts', shithead: you fuck, you pay. Next time – er… well maybe not next time but… Look, if you hadna been such a tight cunt, bought her a meal before you shoved your cock up her… then maybe…" He shrugged his shoulders and laid his palm out under the John's rheumy nose.

Yeah, old Johnny Boy worked through them in no time. For a couple of months he was crazy with the possibilities: no sooner had he dumped than he was caught up in the potential of some new configuration. With the exception of Cashmere, he gave each of them at least one go. But it wasn't long before he settled on a few favourites and pretty much left the others alone.

Dreams of Amputation

As it turned out, one of those few was a rogue breeder, originally destined for the labs, who had somehow ended up in Ham's rooftop playground. Johnny suspected something wasn't quite right with her from the start, and singled her out for that very reason.

She played the game like she meant it, played it like it wasn't a game; she was a tradition. For all he could tell she had genuine warmth. He couldn't pinpoint exactly what it was that distinguished her displays of affection from those of the others, but he was sure of a difference nonetheless. She was cursed with a caring nature (they all thought so): a functionally bankrupt piece of devilry courtesy of some impish bio-designer. What else were they to think? They didn't know Ham was packing drowners. The nurturing was her kink; it had to be. Her homely body sure wasn't boasting any special features: her tits sagged, her arse sagged, her knees were knobbly out of high-heels, and her genitals showed no sign of attention whatsoever. None of them had ever met a breeder before, and nobody they knew had ever met one either, so it is no real surprise that she wasn't spotted sooner.

Johnny favoured her over the rest, and even named her. He called her Rose. He thought the name reflected her demeanor, her "antique wurf". She was the only one he allowed down into the main part of the building. She felt guilty about it when she thought of the other girls, but the pleasure outweighed any reservations. She felt as if she was closing in on her destiny, and indeed she was, every gut-blending moment of it. He felt at ease in her company, and such ease was not something he was accustomed to. At first he'd been drawn to the phony adoration of her fellow concubines: he recognized it as something he couldn't trust and it felt like home. But eventually he gave in to her unerring honesty, and she became one of the few friends he had ever had.

His gestation was brief. It was all there implanted in his head. Johnny plumbed some into her and the signs were there within a week. He managed to ignore the projectile vomiting and the sudden deadening of her body's sensitivity, but when the softening stage began he was forced to confront what she was and what he'd done to her. She withdrew to that stupefied contentment common to all completion-stage breeders. He had two months to mourn her before she died. She was all canned smiles and flushed cheeks; her velvety reassurances the work of a nobbled brain nearing its end.

There were storms the night of Johnny Junior's exit. The sky cracked and burned and threw itself onto the grey earth. None but the Watchers witnessed its staged calamity in full. But the sound came to all but the deaf and the dead. Rose's first scream was obliterated, reduced to a silent horror-mauled yawn. Her second found a gap in the night's stridulous percussion and Johnny came running from the next room.

A few minutes later Johnny was poised to crush her skull and put an end to her torment when, her brain suddenly drowned in dopamine, she became still and serene. He watched as her reward centres put the calm on her, only to reveal their empty motivation in the shape of her wide, dead eyes.

He left the baby to its midnight breakfast, and headed for the roof. That night Johnny fucked the silver-spooned shit out of the equine toff and, disappointed at not being able to cum, and with his cock still buried up her arse, blew her face across the floor with Ham's vintage Luger P08. He did for 3 more on sight {(1) A black patent-leather skinned contortionist with blue single-toned eyes and webbed feet got the barrel up her snatch and dropped with the splits. (2) Cashmere got thrown into his path and quickly found his thumbs in her eye sockets and his right boot on her windpipe. The rhythmic bulging of her knickers was still going strong long after he'd crushed her last breath. (3) An octopus-headed bondage model lay spread-legged on the floor in front of him, her suckered dreadlocks peeling and unpeeling skin. He blew a hole through each of her tits, and turned his back on her, a bedraggled starfish floating peacefully on a red pond.} and was nigh on brio-dipped for massacring the rest when, suddenly drained of purpose, his hand slid free of the gun and he walked out.

Before retracing his steps he attempts to mark the tunnel wall with a screen blotter. It leaves no trace. He tests it on the back of his hand. A black line emerges. He tries the wall again but with no success. He attempts to scratch the wall instead, but his ID ring isn't up to it; no matter how hard he pushes the surface remains unmarked. Finally, he gives up and just leaves the blotter on the floor at the base of the ladder.

His spine feels like it has knots in it. Every so often these knots seem to tighten and he's forced to stop and process the pain. When the attacks become more frequent, and the time it takes him to recover from each one lengthens, he is reduced to a near standstill. In the end he has no choice but to lie down and wait for his condition to improve. The lights sear through his eyelids; he flips over onto his belly and rests his face in his palms.

When he comes to he's been digested by the dark. The absence of illumination is complete. He gets to his feet and starts moving. But no lights hail his steps. He takes some comfort in the sound of his breath and the hollow banter of his footsteps.

And then...

And then, as if preying on these former reassurances, the sounds stop. He forms words and noises, stamps his feet, clubs the walls with the sides of his fists, but nothing comes back to him bar the flinching configuration of the walls. He doesn't know which is the lie: the silence or the tangibility. Initially, he's led to mistrust the absence, but as he accustoms himself to his pared-down environment he begins to point his invisible finger at whatever presence is left. He stands, stooped over, hands pinned to the tunnel beside him: the modern picture of crucifixion; Descartes on the cross, paying the price for his non-belief, clutching at the possibility of nails for as long as he can.

And then...

And then the walls expand and leave him floating. His arms fall to his sides and just to feel his hands knock against his legs is enough to get through the next few seconds. He feels his fingers digging into his thighs. He's clinging. After everything, here he is white-knuckling what's left, holding on to an old future like the calendar markings of dead men.

And then... something near him and yet... his thoughts on the run again...

In one of the few remaining prefab taphouses left in the city, Nolan and Grice sit arched into the bar.

"You boys in enforcement?" asks a man sat to their right.

"Why not. Anything you like," says Grice.

"I don't deserve that." He has a cheap generic humanoid model 5 on his shoulders – an early one, with a fucked voicebox that makes every word sound like it's been clawed from rock. "You've assumed me wrong," he continues, staring at the side of Grice's head. His eyes are cut and set wide open, their corneas nacreous and as mutable as the advertisements, lurid and effulgent, that dress the bar and the otherwise sallow faces of its cadre of pissheads.

"It's possible."

"What, you think I was born here? Born brain-wet and bone-soft. That what you think?"

"No, you were born in a manger," says Nolan, not bothering to turn his head, "I read a book about it once."

"Recognition at last," says the man, leaning forward to get a better look at the interjector.

"Don't let it go to your head," says Grice.

"Not much chance of it staying there if it does," says Nolan.

Grice laughs.

"Cheap shot. My connections are solid. That's what matters."

"You're doing fine," says Grice; "I can see that."

"Laugh it up. Fucked if I care. If you'd seen the shit I've seen..."

"That right?"

"No way you're ex-services; I can always tell. You ain't seen shit."

"Fuck do you know. I've seen plenty, and some of the worst of it came courtesy of war heroes like you," Grice says, turning to Nolan and back again.

Nolan is motionless.

"What's the worst you've seen? Come on; let's hear your saddest tale."

"Go get your thrills somewhere else."

"Tell him! Whatever it is, tell him!" says Nolan.

Grice turns to Nolan, who doesn't turn to face him.

"Okay. Okay, I'll tell him."

"So let's hear it then," says the man, repositioning himself on his stool in preparation, his throat soughing.

"You ever heard of Tantalus?"

"No."

"He was a Greek king tortured in Hades. He put the gods' omniscience to the test by feeding them with his own son's flesh. They noticed. His punishment was to stand, ruined with thirst, in water that receded every time he reached for it."

"That's a fucking myth. That didn't happen to anyone, let alone you."

Grice smiles. "So you going to let me tell mine in my own time, or you going to keep pushing?"

"I'm a rodent less a squeak."

"Now part of that I believe," says Nolan.

Grice starts up before the man has time to take offence: "There's this girl, can't have been more than six, out in the Homelands about a year back. I get the call to check over the bungalow of this couple of crank paranoids who'd become convinced that their thoughts were being broadcast across one of the major TV networks. Story is they'd travelled to the network's headquarters and kidnapped three executives in an office, before cutting them into pocket-sized pieces and throwing them out the window. They cut their own throats before anyone could get to them. Anyway, I'm dispatched with my partner to take a look over their place and to pull anything that might go some way to explaining this shit. So I go in, start rooting around in drawers, checking computer files, et cetera, when I notice that one of the doors is bolted and padlocked top and bottom. When we get the door open there's this girl, their daughter, sitting on the floor with a green blanket over her legs. The room's pretty much empty. There's a pile of rubbish in one corner, old food wrappers and water bottles mostly, some books lying about and an empty cage. She looks gaunt, and nervous about us being there. I wonder about the small cage, why it's empty, and about how long she'd been in there. I move closer to her and she holds the blanket down tight. We both try to calm her down, but the panic's set in and she's rigid. Legs are quivering. She's a mess. I ask her about the cage, about how many hamsters she had in there. Eventually, she tells me she has gerbils, two of them, named Mifleh and Adhub. Told us her dad had insisted on the names. Anyway, when the medical team gets there and we finally manage to prise that blanket from her bony little fists we find Mifleh and Adhub underneath, living inside the chewed out muscle of her thighs."

"That it?" says the man, genuinely surprised.

"That's it," says Grice.

"That isn't anything."

"She'd been there for over a month, lonely and neglected, and rather than see her only companions starve she'd picked away at the skin on her legs and encouraged them to eat. That's something."

"That's pathetic."

"For an adult, maybe. For a child it's… it's heartbreaking." Grice is embarrassed by the word and it shows.

"You're the child," says the man, laughing – the modulation of his amusement raw and berserk.

Grice picks up his drink and studies Nolan's face in a mult-angular mirror partially obscured by variously coloured optics; its features appear perforated: eyes dripping into rutted cheeks, mouth secreting black tongues amid teeth spilling like shingle. Discomposed, he grabs Nolan by the shoulder.

"What?" says Nolan, atrabilious, his face dulled but coherent.

"Nothing… I thought I saw… nothing; it's nothing."

"You ready to hear something that'll really break your heart?" says the man, dropping his head to the bar in an attempt to gain eye contact with Grice.

Reluctant to talk, Grice shrugs his shoulders by way of acceptance.

"I promise you when you hear this you're gonna wish you'd declined."

"I already do."

"Nonchalance is a luxury afforded to the ignorant. You'd do well to make the most of it. Believe me, you'll come to miss it."

"You finished?"

"Okay. Okay, so second year in and I was turning clans and claiming heads in every fringe terrain worthy of mention. Same tired old shit the world over. Little edge to it by then. Things went smoothly, and each day arrived a little duller than the one before. We'd had some times in the first six months or so, got our taste of blood. But we propagated the dread so well we put ourselves out of business fast. Truth is we came to miss it. Roped in for the crop, made easy by our early efforts, we soon became weary. The monotony was a killer, and it wasn't long before we started looking for any excuse to break it, manufacturing resistance out of a grumbled word, a sneer. So, anyway, we're out on patrol this particular day – five of us: Bruno, Langstrom, Clay, Turk and myself – and we happen on this broken down settlement; there's about four shacks in all, each lashed together using the bodywork of various cars and an assortment of harvested tree parts. Presuming it empty, we just start on demolishing the place, to no end other than passing the time. The walls came down easy, and we'd all but finished when Clay drags out a man and a young boy. They'd seen us coming and hidden in the back of one of the shacks. Langstrom wanted straight in and started clouting the father and fondling the boy as soon as he laid eyes on them. Turk pulled him off, consoled the boy, put him at ease, and gave the father a damp cloth to tend his nose and mouth. Said he had an idea. I believe a Russian man once saw art in ideas like the one Turk had that day."

"Men see art in everything they do," says Nolan staring into his mutilated reflection; "Not that many make the effort to put it there."

"Indeed. You're right there. Well, artistic or not, Turk's idea came to be. Turk had us sedate the father while he took the boy off for a chat. He managed to convince the boy that his father had been infected, and that if he didn't receive medical treatment immediately he would die. He told him that a worm was eating his father's insides and that it needed removing, that it had already swollen to the size of a snake, having consumed some of his organs. The boy was horrified. Turk asked him if he'd like to help them take it out, help save his dad's life. He agreed, of course, so Turk sent him off in search of a big stick. When they returned the father was still unconscious. Turk rips off the man's shirt and starts cutting into his belly with a knife. Then he delves in with his fingers and pulls out a piece of small intestine. "Got it!" he says, cutting it in two and handing one end to the boy, allowing the other end to slip back into the man's body. He tells him to slowly start pulling it out and winding it around the stick. "We don't want it to snap off inside," he says. Right on cue the dad starts coming round. The look on his face. The look. Watching his son diligently reeling up his guts. How we didn't laugh, I don't know. I really don't."

"So this is the funniest thing you've seen or the worst?" says Grice, humourlessly.

"Might be both. But if you want to talk about sights that claw into your heart, you'd have to go some to top that boy's face struggling to make sense of his father's screaming. Pop's hollering at him to stop while Turk's in his ear, voice soft and gentle, encouraging him to be strong. The boy even starts explaining about the worm, relaying Turk's words about how it'll be out soon and how everything will be better. And then, when his old man's on the way out, his breathing dangerously shallow, and we all start pissing ourselves laughing, he senses something's wrong. Even after Turk tells him the truth he still doesn't stop winding – not straight away. The poor little fucker can't take it in. He's destroyed. And then he starts trying to feed it back in, the fat red worm, his tiny hands frantic, howling like I've never heard. Excruciating, I don't mind admitting."

Grice takes a drink from his glass.

"Well?"

"What did you do with the boy?"

"We let Langstrom have him. Right, that's me. I can't wait any longer." Ruined for the piss, he slips off his stool. He steadies himself, and has to wait a few seconds for his legs to stiffen before pushing himself off in the desired direction.

"Garrulous cunt, ain't he," says Grice.

"Yeah, the man's a real fucking joy," replies Nolan, his every syllable worn. "Back in a minute." He gets up from his stool and follows the man into the toilet.

Miasma of ammonia and butyric acid. Pale walls with the look of sick skin coated in muck sweat and ink. Floor wet and smeared with stretched footprints. A series of relieved mewls issue from a body slumped into the trough.

"Cokey!" says Nolan.

The man turns, his right foot slipping on the floor. He collapses farther into the trough as a pale arc ends its trajectory on his trousers and shoes.

"You're familiar with the name then."

Back upright and fumbling with his fly, his voice deserts him.

"That's the only thing you've ever said worth listening to."

"How do I know you?"

"And now you're spoiling it."

"Was it the story?"

"Craven to the end."

"I couldn't have stopped them even if I'd wanted to."

"Did you want to?"

"It's hard to remember."

"It's not the story."

"Then what? Where do I know you from? I should know you, right?"

"Know me or not, it's no matter."

"But you know me."

"I know you," says Nolan, his smile seemingly buried by the rest of his face, an intaglio dish in a perpetual state of fading.

Cokey, nowhere near as lissom as Nolan, is unable to avoid the metal fist impatiently seeking residence inside his face. Its fleshier counterpart replaces it within the second. Cokey falls back into the trough as the onslaught continues. Nolan can feel the head yielding in ways common to artificial anatomies: he's sensible of his knuckles sinking farther into his skull with every blow, macerating the skin and denting the cranium ever deeper toward its own inner surface. Cokey's legs are in spasm, his arms hanging limply at his side, into the trench, up to the wrists in static piss. Nolan's fists don't let up, mashing Cokey's napper until pliable enough to fractionate, at which point Nolan reverses his momentum, ripping and gouging the imploded remains until he hits wet intersections of neck.

The head in pieces around him, he stops. His arms are shaking with exertion. He crouches and wipes his hands on Cokey's shirt, pulling the fabric between his fingers with a painstaking precision, losing himself in the noiselessness while he can.

"Come on, let's go," says Nolan on his return to the bar.

Grice stands up and finishes his drink. He thinks on asking about the whereabouts of their vaporous narrator, but, with Nolan already heading for the door, follows him out in silence, a silence that neither finds reason to disrupt till much later.

Outside, the trees are rooted into the sky, their bare branches all mapping the same dead-end. The birds fly on their backs beneath the packed soil of cremated bones, whistling firebrands of joy and endless summer days to deaf men in wet rags. Anthills riot in the warm breeze, their queens made supper for a million black mouths eschewing their soft servitude beneath saints on horseback sneering down at the smiles of plum-eyed infants and their weathered mothers. The tortured screams of pig-tailed brides haunt the empty billboards that lay hidden alongside a seemingly endless stretch of punctured fencing. Lonely men conscript new friends from the roadside and practice origami with their skin, folding into existence ancient birds of paradise and shocking red bouquets...

And then, just as his fingers lose his leg and then each other the lights and the tunnel are back. He hears a snuffling sound beyond the tunnel wall and his return is complete. The spatial stabilizers are shot; that much he'd gleaned. He's actually glad to be back. I'm not ready, he thinks. He needs to get back to his container and have the script assimilate his revelation before it happens again. He must streamline his data feed and tell the others to follow suit.

Will I be able to explain it to them, to myself? he wonders. He carries this doubt into the waiting light.

Grice's call came in at 06:30, by which time Nolan had already been awake and dressed for nearly two hours.

"I know it's early, but..."

"I'm up. What is it?"

"You have to see this. I've only just arrived myself. The concierge called it in just after six, and..."

"Called what in? Grice? Hello?" Nolan can hear raised voices, but can't make out what is being said.

"Sorry. The concierge is shitting his pants here. The boys have arrived now; they're taking care of him. The guy's a mess, can't keep his tongue in his head."

"Where are you?"

"Shit. Yeah. Sorry. We're over at Sybaris6."

Nolan ends the call, quickly looks in on Jenny, who is still asleep, and enters the lift.

He'd wanted to catch Jenny before she left for work, and so he hopes, for Grice's sake, that this incident really requires his presence; Grice's tone and disjointed relay of the pertinent information indicated that in all likelihood it did.

He has things that he needed Jenny to hear. They'd have to wait till she got home from work, but he can't stop running through this long-overdue confrontation: his demands that she resign her position, the concessions that he is willing to make in return, relocation strategies, and numerous other plans for their future away from where they are.

Nolan is still playing out this internal dialogue when he pulls up outside Sybaris6, a gargantuan block of a thousand luxury apartments situated just north of the city perimeter.

The car park is teeming with vehicles and city authorities: law enforcement, ambulances, doctor's cars, government officials, contamination squad...

Nolan is barely out of the car when Grice starts calling him over to the service door, situated a good fifty metres from the crowded disarray of the main entrance.

"Who called all this lot?"

"Must have been that crazy fucking concierge; I think he called every bastard number on his emergency contact list. What I want to know is why the fuck he'd call him?" Grice points over Nolan's shoulder at a van marked Stems the Florist just pulling up alongside a row of police cars.

"Jesus fuck! What's it like in there?" asks Nolan.

"We've managed to contain most of them in the foyer and the car park."

"Most?"

"I've let some doctors up, some of our own, of course, and a few others that I didn't have the rank to stop."

"Okay. So what is this thing anyway? How many dead?"

"None. We're still finding them, but they're not dead. Bout as lively as corpses, though."

Grice shuts the door and leads Nolan into a service elevator. "We might as well start on the first floor; they're all in the same state."

"Which is?"

"As I said, they're alive, but they're completely unresponsive. Stiff and staring like statues. The concierge first got concerned when the porters told him that none of the early breakfast orders had answered the door. He tried phoning them and knocking on their doors, but didn't get any joy, so he entered one of the apartments and found a husband and wife sitting completely rigid at their dining table. He checked a couple more apartments, and finding the occupants in the same state embarked on his phoning frenzy."

"And it's the same story throughout the building?"

"All of the ones we've checked so far. Not the staff, mind you. It's only those inside the apartments. We've done about a third of them, and nobody's expecting the rest to be any different."

"And the other buildings in the area?"

"All the surrounding blocks are fine."

The lift eases to a stop and the doors open. Sitting in the hallway dozing, with his feet resting on a breakfast trolley and an empty plate perched precariously on his lap, is Smithson.

"You're not telling me he is on anyone's emergency contact list," says Nolan unable to hide the full measure of his disdain.

"He arrived not more than ten minutes after me. Apparently, his area of medical expertise is conditions of stasis – it figures, right. The medical authorities informed him straight away."

"Well let's not wake him up just yet."

They walk into an apartment across the hall from where Smithson is seated, and gently close the door.

"Which room?" asks Nolan.

"This is the last apartment the concierge checked. They're through here in the bedroom." Grice walks on ahead, opens the door to the bedroom and stands aside and waits for Nolan to enter.

"Shit! No wonder that concierge of yours was in such a state."

"Not the prettiest are they."

"No. No they're not," says Nolan distractedly as he checks the windows and the air vents.

After making a cursory investigation of the room and its contents, he refocuses his attention on the old couple lying naked on the bed. The man is spread-eagled on his back, his mouth wide open. The woman is lying on her side with her knees tucked up into her belly.

Nolan presses his finger into the underside of the man's wrist. "So this is representative?" he asks.

"Well, most of them are either sitting or laying down, if that's what you mean, but there's nothing particularly uniform about the way they're sitting or laying."

"And you haven't found any puncture marks on the bodies?"

"I've had the docs give them a thorough checking over and nothing yet. There's always the chance that they've been poisoned. Maybe there's something in the water."

"It's possible. Have someone check the building's reservoir."

"Someone's already on it."

"Also, I want the air filtration units checked. All ventilation points need to be checked for residue."

"Gassed?"

"We need to eliminate the possibility, case somebody else thinks of it."

"So what do you think happened?"

"What makes you so sure it isn't still happening?"

"I don't see how…"

"Exactly my point: until we have the 'how' we can't really say much else. I suppose we might as well hear what that odious turd in the hallway has to say. Would you do the honours?" Nolan flicks his head in the direction of the front door of the apartment.

Grice leaves and returns moments later with a muzzy-eyed Smithson scratching at an egg stain on the front of his shirt.

"Enjoy your breakfast?" asks Nolan.

"You should have alerted me when you arrived."

"Sorry about that, but I thought you'd come down with this sleeping bug."

"They're not sleeping. And it isn't a bug."

"Enlighten us, by all means," says Nolan, pleased that he'd been able to antagonise Smithson so easily.

"Well, I ran some tests when I arrived, and they are very much awake, although not responsive to their surroundings in any way."

"What do you think caused it?" asks Grice.

"He doesn't know," says Nolan, walking away towards the couple on the bed.

"I know that you could stand there looking at those two

for a year and still be none the wiser. I know that much, Agent Nolan."

"So do you know what is wrong with them or not?" asks Grice.

"I have a hypothesis that is, as yet, proving resilient to falsification; so yes, I believe I do know what's wrong with them." Smithson looks over at Nolan hoping for a reaction.

Nolan remains as still and indifferent as the elderly bodies on the bed.

"You plan on sharing it?" asks Grice.

"Of course. But I don't report to you. Any findings I make have to go through my superiors, and then they pass on to you whatever they deem necessary. You will know as much as they want you to know."

"You hear this shit?"

"I hear it," says Nolan, unperturbed; "what did you expect?"

"I don't know; I thought maybe the acting medical examiner might just share his findings with the people whose job it is to sort out this fucking mess."

"We all have codes of conduct that we have to adhere to. You'd have me break mine, would you?" says Smithson, relishing his moment.

"I'd have you break something," says Nolan, casually.

"Red is the colour of a target, Agent Nolan. Some friendly advice: try not to see red."

Nolan turns to face Smithson. "How long will they stay like

this?"

"I can't give you the exact duration, but I don't think their present condition is a permanent one."

Nolan turns to Grice. "I want to see some other apartments, unopened ones."

They leave Smithson standing in the doorway eyeing an untouched breakfast trolley that has been left outside an adjacent apartment.

After another hour or so Nolan is forced to admit that Smithson was right: he could look inside every single apartment, pour over their contents for years, and he still wouldn't glean anything that'd help explain the block's sudden mass stasis. Smithson is obviously in a position to deduce a cause from the symptoms alone. The only thing that Nolan can guarantee with any certainty is that the sooner the residents of Sybaris6 return to normal functioning the easier it would be on him, and the quicker he can drive home and talk to Jenny.

"I think we should try and force the issue a little," says Nolan.

Grice can't take his eyes off the middle-aged male resident sat on a sofa in the corner of the room hunched over his breakfast bowl, mouth half open coddling an un-masticated slice of banana on his tongue.

"Is Harris still on this floor?" asks Nolan.

"Yeah, he's about three back."

"Get him in here! I want to try something."

As soon as Grice leaves in search of the doctor, Nolan moves the table back away from the man on the sofa, and sits down on it facing him.

He wrenches the spoon from his hand, and scoops the banana slice out of his mouth, as a precaution against choking. Collecting up a fold of skin from the man's forearm in between his thumb and forefinger, he pinches as hard as he can.

The man does not even flinch.

Nolan kicks the point of his shoe into the man's bare shin. His foot shifts back with the impact, but Nolan can see no other reaction.

He waits a moment, listening for footsteps, and hearing nothing gives the man a hard slap around the face. His upper body rocks to the left and rocks back again; his eyes do not blink and his breathing does not hasten.

Nolan stands up and goes and sits at the dining room table.

Minutes later Grice returns with Harris.

"Good to see you again," says Harris on entering the room.

"Likewise. Thanks for coming."

"Glad to. Nothing routine about this one, eh?"

"Do you have any adrenaline shots on you?"

"Not on me, but I can get some sent up from the wagon."

"Would you?"

"Sure." Harris goes out into the hall to make the necessary arrangements and on returning pulls out a seat at the dining table across from Nolan and sits down.

"You want me to stick one in him?" asks Harris looking at the man on the sofa.

"I want you to stick as many in him as it takes."

"As what takes? You want him to move, dance a jig, what?"

"We'll see."

"I'm willing to try one, but any more than that and you'll have to get someone else."

"Okay, we'll stick to one and see what happens."

An ambulance carrier turns up at the door about five minutes later. "Who's signing for the epinephrine?" he asks in a surly tone.

Harris signs the sheet and sits down on the table in front of the sofa. After prepping the syringe and the man's vein he slides the needle into his arm and plunges its contents home.

After extracting the needle, Harris gets to his feet and begins edging back, away from the sofa.

"You expecting him to go off?" asks Nolan.

"I'm not sure how he'll react; I don't like not being sure."

All three of them stand watching.

Nothing happens.

Nolan begins muttering something about further doses.

"You remember what I said about any additional injections…"

"Wait! Look!" says Grice.

"What? I don't see anything," says Nolan, now alongside Grice, his face inches away from the static man's bloated nose.

He turns to Harris and asks, "How long for it to take effect?"

"There we go. His eyes. Look!" says Grice.

The man's eyes have turned a deep red, and the veins in his arms are fattening up and threatening to burst out through the skin. A few seconds later and he is quaking all over, as if a series of explosions are going off inside him. They all watch as he collapsed in on himself, his skin shrinking to the bone as if he's being vacuum-packed.

"Well now you know what happens," says Harris, making his way out of the apartment. "Tell me when you've finished here, and I'll have him collected and taken away for analysis."

"Right. Will do," says Grice, in place of Nolan, whose thoughts are elsewhere.

The rest of the day yielded no new leads, but plenty of questions and complications, and it is after 20.00 when Nolan finally returns home.

Jenny isn't in.

On the drive back, Nolan had convinced himself that she would have chosen to work the day-shift, and so would be back by seven, seven-thirty at the latest. Her absence comes as a savage disappointment.

He isn't prepared to wait it out. He makes for his wall-safe and takes out a vial of sleeping pills. There are only five left. He takes one, vowing to replenish his supply as soon as possible, and lays down on the bed to await the effects. Sleeping pills are high on the list of banned substances, and procuring them is not without difficulty, even for Nolan, so he makes sure to save them for occasions when he cannot bear to stay awake. That night qualified.

○

The station is full of copies, thought-structures all breathing the same boxed air as him, screwed down into new estates, their borrowed movements vapour trails of the imperceptible multitudes that precede them, his forced embodiment a shriek he cannot hear, its explicit exclusion of human context conveyed in a series of smirks and titters causing him to wake repeatedly inside glimpses of himself, a reluctant conduit to spasms outside the insulation of a body, some dead agent without a face and him mad yellow escaping his dismembered endurance, expanding into nothing in the artificial disfigurement of their smiles until he finds an unsecured staircase, and unaware of any alien intent they carry it up after him, hands formed like mouths barking, their dreams of souls all shrunken cages in its swarm of dead beginnings, their every defect growing into holes, and up into the street and they disperse around him their brains once again made of the digitalised ooze of money and fucking and blood, his own voice coming back removed as if from a TV in another room, his limbs appendixes to an earthquake camouflaged by some Sadean baptism of puke and shit, and nothing and no sound, its hold fixed on the ends of unpronounced words, agitating images of string, an animated ossuary squeezed with rainless faces shining like simulated sick…

When Nolan wakes from his artificially-induced sleep, he does so slowly, painfully. He always has to pay the price for his easy annihilation. The first hour is the worst, the gradual return to self feeling every bit like fortifying a curse.

Jenny is not in the bed, and the mattress beside him is cool and flat.

"Jenny," he shouts.

Nothing.

He struggles to his feet and scours the apartment.

She isn't there. Nolan knows where she'll be, at least he hopes he does, because if she isn't there chances are she isn't anywhere. She always comes home after work, so she is either still at work or she is dead. Those are the only two options Nolan can come up with.

Jenny works in North Block on Spectre Field Park, not ten minutes drive from their apartment complex. Nolan pulls up at the barrier separating him from the Block's parking facility.

"Let the camera see your pass," says the security guard from inside the kiosk.

"I was here last month and the month before that. Don't you recognise me?" replies Nolan.

"No I don't. It's part of my job not to recognise people. That's how mistakes are made."

Nolan flashes his ID to the camera trained on the car.

"Okay, go through. Please report to reception."

The barrier goes up, but Nolan stays put.

"Why are you even here? What purpose do you serve?" asks Nolan, equal parts annoyed and intrigued.

"I'm a human face."

"Not quite," mutters Nolan as he drives through into the car park.

He pulls up outside the entrance to the building and gets out, not bothering to position his car into one of the demarcated parking slots.

"You can't leave your car there, sir," says the woman behind reception in an officious tone.

"It'll stay there until I leave, so the sooner you…"

"You'll have to move it right away, sir. All cars must be parked inside the designated parking zone."

"Is that your brother out there in the kiosk?"

"My brother? I don't understand, sir. I was talking about your car. It really can't stay there."

"Agent Nolan!" says a voice behind him.

Nolan turns around to find two men dressed in identical grey suits standing side by side sharing a smile.

"Don't tell me my car is bothering you as well."

"Your car, no, Agent Nolan, your car is of no concern to us.

We were going to contact you, but when we received word that you had already left your building we thought we'd wait for you here. If you follow us we'll explain everything."

The other man, the man on the right, nods in approval of what his colleague has said.

"I'm not here for a chat," says Nolan.

"No, you are here to collect a Ms Jennifer Sprill, and we are here to provide you with the information you require, so if you'll follow us." They both turn and walk past the reception desk into the main body of the building.

Nolan follows.

Three security-sealed doors later and Nolan is being offered a hard plastic chair in what looks like a small conference room. The two men wait for him to sit down and then follow suit at the opposite end of the square table.

"I thought we were going to see Jenny."

"We will, but first it is incumbent on us to explain the situation," says the more loquacious of the two men.

"Situation?"

"I'm afraid we have some rather unfortunate news, Agent Nolan, news relevant not only to yourself, but news that will also have to be delivered to many others over the next few hours."

"Company's no comfort to me."

"No of course not. I wasn't…"

"So just explain; you said you had something to explain: explain it!"

"My colleague has the details, so I'll pass over to him." He turns to the other man, and they exchange smiles.

Turning back to Nolan, his face now tight with seriousness, the other man starts talking: "The situation as it stands is this: yesterday morning at precisely twelve minutes past eleven an anomaly occurred, not only in this block, but across SFP as a whole, an anomaly about which I can provide only consequent details, the crux of which is that every single one of our Spectre8s is locked in harness to the network. I regret to inform you that Ms Jennifer Sprill was working at the time the anomaly occurred."

"How are they locked? In harness how?"

"We're not sure, Agent Nolan, but what we are sure about is what happens if that harness is breached."

"Which is?"

"I believe you've had first-hand experience of what happens: yesterday at Sybaris6 with a Mr. Armitage."

"Was that his name?" says Nolan, absentmindedly.

"Yes, that was his name."

"Who has time for the names of the dead?"

"But unlike Mr. Armitage's death, which was initiated with an injection of epinephrine, our unfortunate fatality was occasioned by us merely obscuring the screens from a Spectre8's view."

"A Spectre8?"

"We'd prefer not to divulge a name at this stage."

"From what I've heard you prefer to do without them altogether."

"We share some common ground, then, Agent Nolan."

"So what's happening? How long before the connection can be broken?"

"Nobody can say. We lack the necessary information to make any sort of predictions regarding the duration of this phenomenon."

"So you plan to keep Jenny here indefinitely."

"It is not a matter of us keeping Jennifer here, Agent Nolan. You must understand that we have no choice: she remains active in her booth or she dies; that is the grim truth."

"Just how grim it is depends on where your loyalties lie."

"Are you insinuating that Spectre Field Industries had a hand in this?"

"I'm saying that this won't damage your productivity. I'd like to hear you deny it."

He glances at his colleague and they exchange nods. "We'll ignore that remark, Agent Nolan. In light of the news you have just received I don't feel that it would be appropriate to…"

"To what? Appropriate to what, you oily prick?"

"I'd advise you to modify your behaviour, or you will be escorted off the premises and will not be permitted to return."

"You plan on ejecting a police inspector?"

"You have no jurisdiction here. We are self-governing, self-policed. Your post and rank are meaningless here."

Nolan shifts in his chair.

"This ruling was passed months ago. Were you not informed, Agent Nolan? Or are you simply too busy to keep up with changes in legislation?"

Nolan is not aware of this constitutional tweak, and his dejected silence makes plain that his ignorance of it does in no way provide support for its being spurious.

"Nevertheless, we like to maintain a good relationship with external law enforcement. We do not wish our segregation to in any way incite conflict."

"When can I see Jenny?" asks Nolan.

"As long as you feel that everything has been made sufficiently clear, we can go up now."

Both men look at Nolan, awaiting confirmation.

"It's clear," says Nolan getting to his feet.

"Then let's go," says the other man, leading the way.

Nolan has never seen Jenny at work, and has never wanted to. He needs to see her now, but still feels queasy at the prospect.

She sits in the passenger seat of the car in a lay-by on the edge of the desert. The dunes in the distance roll and glimmer like the snarled tumult in a nest of snakes. Her door is open, and her long brown legs extend free of the car, her heels buried in white ash a metre apart. Her hair is dull and unkempt. Her white, strapless summer dress is covered in hundreds of tiny black insects; they climb over each other in an effort to escape. The sun brands her legs while her face remains hidden in the shade. She leans forward, pulls her sunglasses down onto the end of her blistered nose, and smiles. Her teeth are a pale grey, lustreless and chipped, her eyes dark and lascivious.

"Stop spying on me!" she says.

She places her hands on her knees, closes her eyes and inclines her face toward the sun.

"I don't want you to bring me here anymore," she says; "I don't want you to come here again."

She slides her sunglasses back up over her reddened eyes, and leans back into the relative cool of the car.

Grice calls in his location, and sends his men to mark the exits while he waits for Nolan at the front entrance. Thick red clouds race along the insides of the sky. He drops his gaze: he still gets the motion sickness after all this time. Years of bleeding out degenerate externalists, and still he cannot acclimatize himself to this accelerated shroud. He used to take pills for it, but they wrecked his guts and dulled his senses.

Nolan is on the scene in minutes. He saunters over to Grice, nods his head in acknowledgement, and then slowly tips his head back as far as it'll go. He stands there, legs slightly spread, and watches as the clouds scramble into each other and out of sight in continuous relay.

"Like a waterfall of frothy blood. Where's it going in such a hurry anyway?"

"Wouldn't like to say."

"The old welkin still giving you the greens, eh?"

"Nothing I can do about it. It used to get my old mum the same way."

"Keep tracking those toes then, I guess. So what we looking at in there? Usual? Just going in and letting them know we still care; that it?"

"That and the trackers."

He puts his hand on the door and turns back to Grice. "You boys stay where you are: I'll handle this on my own."

Once inside he heads for the bar.

George's t-girl is slouched across two bar stools nosing in on a couple of bum writers.

"I get the bitch so wet she squirts er juices in me face," says one of the men, his nose in his glass, resting between swigs.

"That'll explain the jaundice, darlin," she says lazily.

"Huh..?"

"Piss dries yellow."

"Ain't no facking piss – it's love juice."

"Darlin, yer girl been pissing in yer face for the past week, it better be." Laughter wriggles through her and she crashes to the floor.

Everyone makes a resolute effort not to notice Nolan's presence, to be natural and legal at the same time – no small task for anyone, anywhere, at any time. The trappers on the mezzanine are a study in nervous defiance, their eyes locking on to Nolan's every move; their glances, when they risk them, are toward the window to their left.

Nolan gets his neckstraw from his pocket and places it on the bar. "Vodka!"

The relief barman plays at being flummoxed. "Only state-sanctioned beers and spirits here, mister."

"Do I look like I drink that shit? This smiling is it?" He taps at the display panel that represents the majority of his mouth.

"Maybe you're due a top-up."

"Fuck off, wanker; just get me my drink."

The barman looks across the faces of the regulars, takes heed of the nodding wallpaper of chagrined faces, and pours Nolan his vodka, filling the tumbler to the top by way of apology.

Nolan drains half his drink and turns to face the room, leaning back against the bar with his elbows as support. Surveying the tables, he deliberately ignores the mezzanine. Recognizing most of the faces he sees, he stares at each of them in turn, waiting till they look up so he can give them his nod of recognition. There are a group of younger guys seated along the wall to the right of him. They're new; he's never seen them before, but he knows what they are.

"Got yourself some new recruits, I see. The doom-peddlers get younger and younger as the truth gets older and older. Whadya reckon, a coincidence you think?" Nobody even considers answering. He laughs. "Howdyu lads get the disease so young? Come on, tell me! Maybe I can help you… No word from the wordsmiths, eh. What a surprise; on a par with finding a Trapper with some brains, that one. Only shitting you, Johnny. Fuck, self-deprecation's quite the thing nowadays; I'm just having me a piece of it." Nolan's pixel gaze stays put. The young poets squirm in their seats. He is addressing the room through them and they feel it. "It damn near puts me on the wrong side of the law looking at you boys; saddens me it does. Fit young men like you, and here you are all brimming with incompleteness and all the new dresses you're planning on draping it in. They're just holes, boys. It don't matter how you gild the edges. Only they ain't even holes anymore. Did nobody tell you? It's been a while I grant you, but as yet no signs of erosion. Your plan was busted before you were even born, you dumb fuckers. It's over: time to stop crying and start living. How can you find meaning in a void that doesn't exist? Futility for its own sake, now there's an idea. Could be something in that you know." He looks around the room and laughs, looking for some eyes to share the joke with.

He doesn't find any.

He turns round and finishes his drink.

The barman quits polishing clean glasses and pours him another.

"A word, Johnny." He shouts, not bothering to turn round.

Johnny can't help but smirk: always the show before business. He takes his time, pride impeding every move he makes. A couple of minutes later – a period suitable to both parties – he arrives at the bar and pulls up a stool.

Nolan has a new customer for him, and he wants his usual cut. The guy is silly rich and sick for the goods. He's told him that Johnny is the best and has guaranteed his satisfaction. He hopes Johnny won't let him down. Johnny takes the address without saying a word. They both know the routine by now, and Johnny waits for Nolan to leave before returning to the mezzanine.

The new customer's name is Hamilton Jones IX.

When he eventually comes across a ladder, the blotter is there waiting for him. The best explanation was always the loop, but he's still holding out.

He doesn't know why.

His instincts are at variance with the facts, and yet, strangely, he feels comfortable with it.

He struggles up the ladder, losing his footing and slamming his chin into a rung on more than one occasion. He smells death as he inches over the top; all the sad stench-laden apologies of man's retreat to flesh creep up his nostrils.

His own excavated body makes for quite a sight: the concertinaed skin rising up from the floor like a pile of dirty washing, around it what remains of the flushed out slush of his insides is forming a crust. Leaning over, the toes of his shoes a good inch away from the muck, he stretches out the crinkled folds of his face. It hangs from his fingers, the very antithesis of caricature. And yet there is no doubt whose face he is looking at. It is the reflection from a nightmare, warped, over-digested, blanched in the horrors of familiarity, unmistakable, its identity prescribed. A duplicate. A good one. Made for purpose. But what purpose? What has been achieved by his watching its mutilation and then finding the residuum in a container that his blotter indicated as being the only container to which the tunnel provides access?

He scans through his security files, checking for breaches. No reports have been logged. He's still bewitched by the zeros when the screens darken. One, two… and there he is clambering out of the shaft into his container. He watches as he clambers to his feet and sets about confirming that the container is indeed indistinguishable from the one he'd just left. He lingers over the floor panel a while, wheels his chair over to the rest area, and leans the floor panel up against the central pillar. He watches himself disappear back down the shaft.

The script returns and he's left wondering, his expectations breeding their own negations.

He cannot deny the fact that he appears to have had a revelation, and he cannot deny the confusion that has arisen because of that. What happened to him in the tunnel? Is the tunnel circular or not? Where did the duplicate come from? Is he the duplicate? He cannot deny that these are questions, and that he doesn't have any solid answers to them. How is it possible for him not to know? If he doesn't know something, it's not there to know.

He shuffles over to the rest area. He needs to get a couple of hours: uncertainty is tiring; he's not built for it. He allows himself to unite with his aching limbs and in what seems like no time he's scrambled beyond all recognition.

Back on the street, Nolan dismisses Grice and his men, and returns to his car. He ports into the controls and she starts up. His thoughts get him home quicker than usual, and as he drives into the underground parking lot beneath his block he's surprised to see that he's the first one back.

Nolan lives in an old recon block situated in the dead centre of the city. His apartment occupies a whole floor. It is almost entirely open-plan, with full glass exterior and a 360° terrace. Nobody down on the street knows he lives in a place like this, or knows of the money he has accumulated since the war. If they found out, his cover would be all the more troublesome. He couldn't realistically mask his intentions with extortion, bribery and the like if the marks knew of the funds at his disposal.

Hamilton had been a real find for Nolan. Bored and rich, the venal little prick was virtually cut from his dreams, so Nolan sold him the taste the old way, without having to resort to the loaded mouth swab in his pocket. He offered to hook him up with someone in a few days, and he just knew that Ham would be dead-timing till Johnny Boy turned up at his door. He was sold on the thought alone, his drenched palm belying any surface cool. Nolan wasn't even sure he'd need the enhancer to finish him off.

The goat's head might be gone, but the connections are the same. Like all the others, Nolan couldn't lose the remote links without losing himself in the process – or to be more precise, losing the self that can walk, talk and experience things beyond the realm of thought. It's hard for any of the old soldiers to think of themselves as divided in this way. They exist where the experience exists; that's all there is to it for most of them. And they are of course right for the most part. But what screws Nolan over is not so much the remoteness of his brain, as the company it keeps. He is not alone in his own head, no ex-serviceman is. For most, whose bodies were destroyed in the war, it is of no great concern: they are glad of the company. And out of those who brought their heads back intact, the vast majority are too concerned with surviving to pay much attention to their psychological privacy. Nolan's intelligence and ruthlessness allowed him to accumulate money and power, and with these he found the time to build obsession, and the one he built the biggest was that of his own internal solitude.

Duplication technologies had seemed a promising route until he saw what happened to the first of the test subjects. The replication process somehow interfered with the signal, triggering security measures within the network: the pioneers' brains were boiled in their vats. It was tantamount to suicide during the period of those early trials, and was not without risk now. But, such dangers aside, even if the procedure proved successful, the transfer could only ever be partial. The degree of recovery was curtailed by time constraints and depth-encryption, and with little hope of overcoming these difficulties, Nolan decided to pursue other less hazardous but rather more speculative methods.

There are moments when he experiences a brief lull in cerebral noise; for just a few seconds he is alone without having to concentrate, and it's these fleeting intervals that are the cynosure of his days. These are the only times he is relieved from reinforcing his boundaries, from shoring up his territory against what is an otherwise constant salvo of wandering ideas looking to make him their new home. Even his sleep is corrupted by half-owned thoughts ingratiating themselves into his dreams. Excluding the momentary glimpses of interior solitude, his vigil is, and needs to remain, ceaseless.

Once inside the apartment his face screens dull and start to blur at the edges; his shoulders slump fractionally as he makes for the terrace. He is tired of many things, but the view from that strip of fenced concrete isn't one of them. He looks out on hundreds of extractor fans spinning dirty air into spotlighted mesh, their batteries glowing like raw blisters on the re-emerging skyline. The tallest of the new tower blocks reach up into the low red sky, as if trying to support its weight. Inside are the lights of an endless world of screens dimming and flashing before a legion of conscripted peepers. Huge patches of bramble-infested waste ground are scattered to the horizon, the eyes of countless species of vermin glinting back at him from the alien undergrowth. The ritualized shrieks of starving cats and malformed humans punctuate the drone of bitter laughter and unwelcome voices that invade every step of Nolan's nightly circuits.

This is a place Nolan understands, a place that he has successfully exploited for decades, and whose inhabitants he finds pleasingly pliable – if only he could extend this lazy dominion to the sanctions of his own mind.

It wasn't long before Johnny came to see his son as an agreeable distraction. Once his conniption over the loss of Rose had passed, he found himself seeking out his son's company more and more frequently. He hadn't reckoned on forging any attachments to the thing, but almost without consultation his emotions, so long ransacked, were furnished with the whimsies of fatherhood.

Dreams of Amputation

He took over his needs completely, relieving the Jocasta doll from her duties as chief care-giver. As doting as she was, it wasn't ideal to have your newborn groomed by its makeshift mother. But he could hardly have blamed her for her design: he could have killed her in an instant and thought no more about it, but what had that to do with blame? What had anything to do with blame?

Little Johnny was precisely 6 months old when they came for him. They came up through the lift-shafts, in through the windows and the roof. They infiltrated the dome from the air, smashing through the glass simultaneously at five points. Watching the seductresses innocently sidling up to their slayers was almost moving, reminiscent as it was of stories told about Dodos and Dutchmen. The peculiarity of their targets gave the ensuing slaughter something of a party atmosphere: there was laughter, shouting, light-hearted banter, rushed promiscuity, head-shots, the sounds of bones being shattered, of fluids hitting walls, of throats gargling cum and then blood. The squad suffered an unnecessary fatality when a young corporal was killed by the 25-foot Amazon: he'd blown her knees to bits and then been distracted by what two of his buddies were doing to the Necro800 on the other side of the dome; the Amazon's peppered torso crushed him flat, his insides jetting out from a hollow in her ribcage for some considerable distance.

Johnny and his son were eating their way through a bag of raw steak when the lights went out. He heard windows blow in down the hallway. He grabbed his son and headed for the armoury. He'd managed just a few strides when a hollow point blew the bottom of his face off. His heart and left lung hosted the transit of two more shots and he dropped to the floor. Little Johnny lay beside him bawling.

When the lights came back on there were men wearing black boiler-suits lining the hallway walls. The last thing Logan saw was a pair of pointed leather shoes approaching him, and the flash of a silver arm reaching for his son.

Nolan pulls into the car park round the back of Lab South5. As he walks toward the building he spots Smithson putting the moves on one of his female technicians. She is taking his advances well, cigarette smoke leaking from her smiles. Seeing Nolan approaching, he whispers something in her ear. She walks off, dragging her cigarette along the wall until nothing but the filter remains.

"What's the opposite of a sexual stimulant, Agent Nolan?" says Smithson.

"I do hate to get in the way of true love, but I need a favour."

"A Nolan favour – here we go."

"Who is it keeps the skin on your back?"

"That card's a little tattered isn't it. Exactly how many outsiders are left? Not many from what I've heard."

"As many as I want there to be. You'd do well to remember that." Nolan's eyes widen in an attempt to soften the threat, to keep things on friendly terms.

"I'm still not convinced that they can get through our defences, however many of them you allow to exist. The last breach was months ago and there haven't been any sightings since. These tail-enders don't have the brains for... they're not organized enough – are they? – for such an operation."

"They have brains enough. You know better than to be complacent."

Smithson's rotund frame needs fortification. His lunch is overdue and he is starting to feel it. He has refused to convert to HB pills, preferring his gustatory satisfactions to be literal. Despite having a busy schedule, he can't imagine why anyone would sacrifice the pleasures of eating, even if it meant having to do it on the job.

"So this favour..."

"I need you to process a Sage for me."

"We're not running any at the moment. The quota's full."

"Fuck the quota; we won't be banking him. I want you to hand him over to me once you've done."

"Shit. You're serious. How am I going to explain it if anyone comes asking?"

"Don't give me that; you know how to ride out the scans. You manage to disguise your visits to the Spectre8s without too much difficulty."

Smithson has a predilection for having sex with attractive young Spectre8s, and Nolan knows all about it, as he is the one who facilitated his visits. The practice is illegal, as is anything that jeopardizes the careful balance of contrived surveillance. Thankfully, the targets of his desire barely know what is going on when he sets on them, for as long as they can maintain visual contact with their screens, they remain almost entirely oblivious to their molestation.

Smithson sniffs another veiled threat. "Maybe, but it takes time, a month or more. Questions will be asked."

"All the more reason to rush it through."

"The quicker we run him the worse he'll feel it, and the worse he feels it, the more likely it is that he'll draw attention to himself."

"Don't concern yourself about that: I have a safe place to keep him. He'll be sealed off, registering a BIG FAT zero." Nolan's eyes linger over Smithson's sludgy midriff.

"There's no such thing as zero."

"I can think of at least one example." Nolan smiles the unfriendliest of smiles.

"Let's dispense with the threats. Anyway, that isn't strictly true. Death won't save you."

"I'll give up on zero when you stop troughing like a pig."

"Insults now."

"I'm restraining myself."

"So when do you plan on bringing him in?"

Nolan tilts his head in the direction of his car. "He's in the boot."

"Okay, let's get him inside; I haven't eaten since breakfast."

They walk over to Nolan's car, Smithson trailing behind, doing his best to subdue what is either a grimace or a belch.

Nolan cracks the boot and stands back to allow Smithson to get a good look.

"Shit, Nolan, he's not even broken 365. We don't do them this young: you risk complications. You're pushing it with this favour."

"Remind me, who was it had to clean up the mess when you decided to get inventive with that young girl in the Delta Stratum?"

"I thought we agreed to... Okay. Wrap him up in that sheet, and follow me."

Nolan swathes the sleeping infant in a corpse sheet and follows Smithson into the lab. Once inside, Nolan has one further favour to ask. He tells Smithson that, in addition to some necessary mnemonic tweaks, he needs the boy to share his need. He feels vulnerable as he says it, especially after the rather tetchy exchange outside.

Smithson finishes his mouthful, forcing the partially masticated bread and salami down his throat with a hard swallow. With his face flushed and his eyes watering, he expresses his reservations: "But that'll mean a scan, and you know the risks with that. I don't get it. I mean, if we're going to go that far we might as well try for cerebral replication at the same time."

"No scan. You'll have to manufacture one. It doesn't have to be a perfect match."

"It won't be; you can rely on that." he says, before filling up his mouth again.

"I can rely on it being good enough though can't I?" Undercurrents of aggression once again present in Nolan's voice.

"Good enough for what?"

"Just give me a Psych-Box, and once I've done you can get all you need from there. The answer to your last question won't appear, but if you really need to look for it then maybe I'd better find someone else."

"It'll mean working late, of course. Okay, okay, I'll do my best. You'll hook me up again when I'm done?"

"I'll do my best."

After rummaging around in a floor-level drawer, Smithson hands Nolan a Psych-Box – a voice-sensitive device for targeting and mapping specific psychological features, the world inside your head there in what comes out of it – and then sets about unwrapping his new test subject.

Nolan returns home just after 20:00. Jenny is already home. She is sitting out on the balcony smoking. She has showered. Her hair is still wet and collected in a knot on top of her head. She looks up and smiles as Nolan comes up beside her and places his hand on her shoulder.

"Early finish?" asks Nolan.

"I was planning on doing the late shift," she says looking away in the direction of the tower blocks.

"But you were in most of the day, weren't you?"

"Only till four."

"Nine out of twenty-four is sufficient, don't you think."

"It wouldn't be till midnight. We have plenty of time before then."

"At least you could take your eyes off the fucking place when you aren't there."

"What? I'm not... I'm not looking at anything in particular. I'll sit like this if you'd prefer." She says, turning her chair to face the wall.

Nolan drops the keys Grice had given him earlier onto the glass-topped table.

The noise startles Jenny out of her slouch.

"I think we should go this time," says Nolan, walking back into the apartment.

"If you go, you'll have to leave that screen behind," she shouts after him.

Nolan watches as the Sage's script falls down the screen uninterrupted. He chooses to ignore Jenny's remark and instead lose himself in what he finds progressively more difficult to see as anything but his own inevitable failure.

Jenny comes in from the balcony and sits behind him on the arm of the sofa, hard and angular and grey and looking better than it felt.

"Well?" says Jenny.

Nolan doesn't answer.

"You complain about my working too much, and then you come home and stare at that for hours on end."

"This isn't me junking time to get money we don't need," says Nolan, turning round, "this is… this is about…"

"It's not about money; it's about feeling useful. You know that. We all need it – even you."

"That's not what I need."

"I know what you need. But it's just a dream. It's been years. If it comes off then great, but… things aren't so bad as they are."

"Grice is right," says Nolan, turning back to the screen.

"Right about what?"

"It doesn't matter."

"It does now. So what is it? What's he right about?"

"This is our only way out: that's what matters."

"To you, yes! The problem is it's become the only thing that matters. Haven't we been happy without it?"

"They're always there."

"But they're quieter now. You said so."

"Till the next time, and I've learnt to defend myself, but I'm tired, they're wearing me down. Genuine respite's rare, and when it does come I spend the whole time dreading its end. I want it to be just us. You and me somewhere else. No voices but our own."

Jenny comes up behind Nolan and puts her arms around his neck. "We'll go. We'll go to Grice's place."

"Fuck Grice's place. It'll only make it worse. I don't know why I thought…"

"We'll go. It won't make anything worse, and we'll be away from here for a while. Next week. We'll go next week."

"And work?"

"I'll make up the hours. I'll go in a little earlier tonight. It'll be fine. And then next week, or maybe the week after, we'll go."

Nolan pulls up outside the container. He waits a few minutes before entering, apprehensive about what he might find.

As he opens the second door into the main living quarters, he finds the Sage laying on his bunk, motionless.

Nolan walks over to him, pulls up a chair and sits down.

The Sage doesn't stir. His blue overalls are unbuttoned to the waist revealing his pale, thin chest.

"Are you awake?" Nolan asks.

"Yes."

"Are you okay to talk?"

The Sage slowly drags himself up into a sitting position, and looks at Nolan.

"Do you know who I am?" Nolan asks.

"Of course. You're the reason I'm alive, the reason I'm here."

"Yes... Well... There are things I need to know."

"Apparently."

"Can you help me?"

"You are driven by love. Rather an antiquated motivation, wouldn't you say?"

"I don't go much on the replacements."

"I find carnal love ridiculous. Don't you think it's about time we sacrificed the lies of furbelowed holes and spatial selves, and freed ourselves from this pitiful bondage?"

"I need you to explain these so-called lies."

"This self-reflexive mirage lies itself into existence; its organizational accomplishments are fact. The mirage gives rise to the reality of delusion, the delusion being the success of the mirage itself. It was here that we found the road to abstraction, and all around it that we found the need. If you subtract the 'here' from the mirage, leaving the 'now' in place, then your consciousness is free to go."

"Where?" asks Nolan, sceptically.

"Nowhere, that's where. You become an abstract being in the very real sense of being a conscious abstraction – the living form of yourself. For the mental representation of non-spatial consciousness can also be non-spatial consciousness; that's the beauty of such a persuasive fiction: it creates what it merely represents, simply in virtue of representing. Once these self-contained snapshots of placelessness have been decrypted and any bugs removed we will have nothing keeping us here but superstition."

"I don't follow."

"That's because you are both hustler and mark: they are one and the same. The hustler does such a good job on himself that even if he realizes how and why he's being conned he can't stop it happening; after all, the unity of mark and hustler have been realized. Even at the time of the revelation he is still lashed to the dupe. The knowledge should allow him to jump free, he thinks, but it doesn't. Why? Because the con is so good it transforms the hustler into the perfect mark i.e. one who does the hustler's work for him. All I propose doing is extracting some unwanted scenery."

"What did you mean by holes? Holes in what?"

"I was talking about the lure of incompleteness, gaps. Objectively, I have all the evidence of its persuasive power. I know the history: I can recall that eventually the arts came to the stage where they did nothing but build its shrine, all of its many disciplines footnoting an elusive emptiness as meaning – the search for meaning transformed into meaning itself. I see the lie. The sense of incompleteness that was often supposed to characterize a particularly modern angst was really our saviour. The sense of an elusive truth or reality that we cannot get a grasp on turned out to be the very embodiment of human hope – widespread self-deception on a par with all the great religions put together.

"On an intellectual level my existence as a Sage, a Knower, stands as refutation. There are no gaps. Whether you give it a face and call it 'God', or leave it in its natural state and nourish in its blankness, the truth remains the same: the salvational void is a beautiful dream that cannot survive the waking eye."

"And you're saying love is one of those gaps."

"Yes. Romantic love is a salvational void, a man-made enigma constructed so as to defy simple encapsulation. Morality is probably the perfect example, and far more revealing when it comes to explaining just who we are."

"So morality has sustained itself all this time on its gaps?"

"In short, yes. Build the gaps into these concepts and let us think we have interests in filling those gaps. Look, morality is undoubtedly a dupe of some endurance, but it isn't the locus of human worth that many took it to be. It's just another distraction, a meaningless riddle that once allowed men to subjugate themselves, thus cutting down on policing, etc. But what most never realize is the real purpose served by morality, and just what it was that stood to benefit from its almost worldwide influence. The moral myth focused humans on their actions, made them responsible for them and the selves from which they originated in a way that no other doctrine ever could. As a tool for strengthening the (already partially realized) delusion of self, it was nothing short of a master stroke. If a parasite wants to establish its independence, then what better way than to make its separateness essential to its host's central system of value. And while the central system of meaning dwindled, finally morphing into something else (its creation, no less), what it had created, what it had been its purpose to create, remained stronger than ever. Morality was a way of creating something that could be moral, and that something wasn't essentially human; it was an abstract controller. It was morality that engineered the self that can no longer be essentially embodied, and the fledgling self that instigated the lie of morality, so it would be fair to say that the self, and the Horde Self along with it, is largely constructed out of the lie of right and wrong. Self for the sake of morality and religious redemption had it the wrong way round."

"By Horde Self, you mean the military mind pool?"

"That was the start of it, yes."

"The start of it? The pool is dwindling not expanding."

"That's the story."

"I'm part of that fucking story," says Nolan, losing his patience with The Sage's ponderous and aloof disclosures.

"I think I best be more detailed in my replies. I am an abstract parasite feeding off a human brain; in this respect I am like all selves. But the parasite, having nowhere better to go ply its trade, gets tied down to this one host."

"Parasite?"

"Yes, but you won't find its signature spinning in a centrifuge."

"So where do you find it? In abstraction?"

"The abstraction that is human psychology, yes."

"Only humans?"

"Like most other parasites, the self is almost perfectly adapted to its host and would die elsewhere. Humans are a self's host."

"What about apes?"

"There are, as you point out, rudimentary selves in, for example, apes and elephants, but they are not the same. They are different flukes entirely."

"I can't see that they're so different."

"I can assure you they are. You only have to think about how the parasite starts off and how it enters its host to realize just how different they are."

"Is this your idea of being more detailed?"

"You must give me time to speak. I am not accustomed to engaging in conversation; there is no call for it in here."

Nolan slides back in his seat, letting this minor chastisement pass.

"Parasites are not created by their hosts; they must enter them from outside. The Horde Parasite entered through language. Without language acquisition there is no means of infection."

"Go on," says Nolan.

"The human body, having assimilated the parasite, seemed loath to let it go. However, the ever-scheming self has been forging the mechanisms of its escape for centuries. For example, consider that feeling of progress that we can't shrug off, and soon you'll recognise yet another masterly grift from the uberself: a world of hijacked bodies toiling to free their hijackers. The self demanded more from its future than fading away in the tired memories of disparate organisms; it needed to retain its unity. The Head Soldiers, of which you were one, became the first members of what was to eventually become the Horde Parasite, or Horde Self: a secret, mass conglomerate of amalgamated selves. The military's BIV database was soon extended to every living being, who no longer had to sacrifice their head and sections of spinal cord, as brain-data transmitters could now be installed at birth. But the Horde Self only cares about the flourishing of its parts insofar as they relate to the whole. Like an anthill it relies on the blind devotion of its many aggregate members to certain behavioural patterns, the full implications of which each member fails to grasp. The utility and glory of the unified subject is not attained by its promoting the utility and glory of each of its parts; what are important are intersections and balance, and the control thereof. Any utility or glory that its parts may come to know is nothing but an extra portion of prison slop. That some sub-parasite happens to bathe in the adoration of his fellow sub-parasites for some allotted period is simply something the optimum configuration demands; its real significance is not something the sub-parasite comprehends, needs to comprehend, or would want to comprehend. A safeguard is in place to prevent us ever doing anything about our predicament even if we should come to realize it. I speak, of course, of the subjective/objective dichotomy – the birthplace of absurdity – which insures that even if some do find out about the relative insignificance of their lives, they are unable to act upon the information. It remains a sterile taunt. The unification of these two ways of viewing ourselves cannot be permitted: the consequences for the Horde Self, and its constituent slave-selves, would be catastrophic.

"Parasitism is just one kind of symbiosis or cohabitation. But the self is a new breed of parasite, neither exclusively an endoparasite, nor exclusively an ectoparasite. The self is present in the human body only in terms of its effects, effects which account for almost all of its physical manifestation: in essence, it is the organising principle, and so abstract, never to be located in space. It is both within and without, and its success lies in its ability to coax its host into making provisions for its transcendence.

"In addition to being characterized in both these ways, it is also a cute variation on what is known as an epiparasite: a parasite that feeds on other parasites. For the self does indeed feed on a parasite, but the parasite on which it feeds is none other than itself, resulting in what is a truly bizarre twist on standard hyperparasitoidism. In order to grow it too must buy into its own existence, constantly fortifying itself, checking for flaws in the circuit that might prove destructive. In fact, the Horde Self has brought a new level of hyperparasitoidism into being, for not only does each self feed on itself, but the collective feeds on its parts, so while it would be foolish to take a stand and side with your body, thus cancelling yourself out, it is scarcely more feasible for you, as a sub-self, to try to extricate yourself from your fellow selves and go it alone."

"And there is no way out."

"There are ways out, but one needs to keep in mind the one very good reason why ants do not isolate themselves from their communities."

"They die."

"They die. But the consequences for us are, initially at least, slightly less dramatic. It is possible to break away and live, but in doing so you sacrifice pretty much all the fabric of the self: every aspect of your identity is infected, integrated into the whole. To break free is to relinquish who you are."

"Like the Heads that severed their connections to the pool?"

"Very similar, yes. Only now the self is likely to be shaved down even further. The Horde Self functions like a fluke, causing its hosts to act in ways necessary to insure its completion, its end-state. If some of its sub-selves have to be sacrificed along the way it is no great sacrifice, and usually no sacrifice at all, given that precautionary measures have been put in place to ensure that any depletion in number can never adversely affect attained levels of psychological richness. It is prepared to become a necrotroph if the benefits are clear."

"So how does it all end?"

"Human-beings and selves have coevolved, each adapting itself to the other. And although the relationship has proved beneficial for both parties up till now, the time has come for the self to make provisions for itself that don't include the individual whims of its long-term hosts. It is now restructuring itself, with only a modicum of regard for the individual interests of each host."

"More extremities of character, less and less balance on the individual human level."

"That's the size of it."

"In order to achieve what?"

"What every other parasite wants to achieve: optimum levels of reproduction."

"The breeding programme."

"The number of breeding labs has doubled in the last year. The numbers will be trebled, quadrupled, and on until any more would incur a deficit through the number of lab workers necessary to maintain the successful running of things."

"This'll result in chronic overpopulation: we'll be crammed together like battery hens."

"There will be a balance. But, yes, I envisage a time when the majority of human beings are confined in tiny pens of some kind."

"Many already are."

"You're talking about Jenny?"

"Yes."

"Things will get worse; I can guarantee that."

"I didn't come here for a prophecy of doom; I came to see if you'd made any headway on a plan to get us out."

"And I have done my best to explain that there is no out – at least not the out that you require."

"To get out we'd have to cease being who we are, forgo all the reasons we… I wanted out in the first place. Forgive me, but this option lacks appeal."

"I realize that this is not ideal for you…"

"Ideal!" Nolan interrupts, spitting the word out like you would a fly.

"But it's the only option there is."

"The only option you can come up with."

"The only option there is."

"I need you to keep looking, keep looking for anomalies, for others.… If you can get out, then maybe…"

"I am nearly ready. But if you find me, you will not like what you find: it will only prove to you what I have told you here today."

"Then why leave so readily?"

"Because unlike you I have grown to hate my encumbrances. I see the purity I speak of as a blessing, a state of pure freedom. Where you see annihilation I see undiluted being."

Nolan gets up from the chair. "Just maybe you are wrong about this one thing. Maybe this is your gap."

"For your sake I might hope so, but for my own I do not."

Nolan replaces the chair in its original position and leaves.

It isn't much of a park, but Jenny loves it. She tries to forget that she has known far superior examples as a child.

It is a delicate balancing act she needs to perform to keep her memories from tainting the present, while still allowing the present to be informed and coloured by the memories of her enjoyment. She is forced to slice her childhood zeal free of its inspiration just enough to permit the present approximation of that inspiration to act as replacement.

It is a popular spot for those with a little free time to use up, and this day is no exception: they arrive and leave in relay, and at any one time all the benches are occupied and most all the imitation grass has lounging bodies on it. The trees at least are real, even if their leaves aren't, but if you don't scrutinise the details you can lose yourself for the short time you are there.

Jenny's favourite place to sit is beside the pond, right at the edge, close enough to dip your hands in the water. She and Nolan sit, cross-legged, and looked across the small expanse of water at two forlorn-looking ducks, their plumage threadbare at best.

"I'll have to get back soon," says Jenny.

"Okay," replies Nolan.

"But thanks for meeting me. I know you don't much care for this place, but… anyway, thanks."

"It's fine. Just like any other place."

"To you, maybe. Just leave it to me to enjoy it for you."

She turns to him and smiles, nudging him lightly with her shoulder.

Nolan doesn't move. He watches the two ducks pecking at each other, and keeps his right arm still with his left. His feet start to twitch and flail uncontrollably. He struggles to uncross them, his head jerking back and forth.

His face screens blur and blacken.

"What's wrong?" says Jenny, as she heaves herself up onto her knees, "What is it? Tell me!"

Light and clarity return to his face, and his body becomes still. He sits, legs stretched out in front of him, his head up facing the sky, both arms out behind him supporting his weight.

"It's nothing...no...thing...every..."

"Come on, let's walk." She stands up and reaches her hand out to him.

"Leave!" screams Nolan as he scrambles to his feet, "Leave!"

He pushes her in the direction of the gated archway that leads back onto the street.

"Go!"

Jenny staggers backwards, refusing to take her eyes off him.

Nolan grabs at his head with both hands and starts pulling at the screens that make up his face.

"Stop it!" Jenny screams, still retreating slowly toward the exit.

Nolan tries to speak, but so do all the rest.

In the end none of them speak: Nolan's voice box cannot

translate the variant thoughts of his many violators. The noise that escapes from his head is less a voice, less a conglomerate of voices, and more the hissing roar of a punctured tyre.

Feeling them closing in on his motor skills, Nolan unclips his gun and throws it into the pond: his last fully lucid act that afternoon.

On the one previous occasion, when his gun had remained on his person for the duration of the seizure, twenty-three people had died. Luckily for Nolan this occurred in a district in which, seizure or no seizure, he would rarely have many qualms about committing a series of random assassinations. But the second time was different: Jenny was present, and in the seconds it took to rid himself of his weapon he offered up thanks to anyone that'd take it for the massacre that had happened through him a little under a year earlier.

He didn't hear the screams or the solicitations ruptured by their own disbelief; he didn't see those eyes blink their last and open blind to the sky, or the softened faces spread across the plastic grass. His body did the work, but he remained absent for most of it, returning only in evanescent glimpses, any mnemonic entrails being readily appropriated by the legion alien selves to which he played host one hour out of that late summer afternoon.

Jenny called Grice, and he arrived with a van and three other men from the squad.

Grice cleared up the mess, just as he had the time before. On this occasion there were only four bodies. However, this could not be confirmed till much later, when all the widely bestrewn parts had been logged and identified.

When Nolan enters his car he finds a message waiting for him.

It's Grice.

"There's been an incident down in the Tubes – Vert 8, subcoil 14, reporting to a Professor Harshaw. No details forthcoming – the typical tight-lipped summons. You know the shit: 'I'm afraid we cannot possibly disclose that information, officer.' Sorry boss, I offered, but they wanted you down there."

"Fucking great," says Nolan, as he stares through his windscreen, out across the cracked road and bleached facades of row upon row of lifeless housing units, "just fucking great."

The Tubes, as the district is commonly known, is a subterranean network of laboratories, a vast concrete warren filled with colourless scientists and their unfortunate test subjects. The studies conducted in that bleak burrow all apparently centred round a common theme: the distillation of terror and misery.

Nolan detests the place.

The drive over there is regrettably short, and as he pulls up Nolan sees Professor Harshaw waiting for him at the entrance to the drop shaft, his hands fidgeting in his lab coat pockets.

"Sooner than expected, Agent Nolan."

"I wanted it over with."

"I'll try not to take offence. There's something you need to see. Shall we go? After you." Nolan enters the elevator and Harshaw follows him in.

A few seconds later they both step out into The Tubes.

"Follow me please."

In the middle of a straight stretch and hearing only his own footsteps, Harshaw turns round to find Nolan's face pressed up against the glass panel of one of a series of lab doors. "Is something the matter?"

"What's wrong with them?" asks Nolan, feigning an interest more detached than it is.

"They are going to die in ten minutes; or at least that's what they believe is going to happen, and quite justifiably. They have some very good reasons to think that their existence is coming to an end, reasons provided by us, of course."

"And what happens when they don't?"

"Oh, that is a revelation that they can never have. They are forever ten minutes away from their deaths. That is, until their final ten minutes ticks out." Harshaw cannot overcome the temptation to smile.

"So they can't feel the passing of time."

"What would be the use of that? The data would be useless. Of course they can feel time passing; what they can't do is make the move from the seemingly normal procession of time, as they wallow in their own dread, to their deadline being overdue. That way their final ten minutes goes on for decades."

"And what have you discovered?"

"I am not in a position to divulge that information. You know that."

"Let me rephrase my question: what do you discover in a lifetime that you fail to discover in the initial ten minutes?"

Harshaw sighs. "We each of us have our areas of excellence for a reason, Agent Nolan. Shall we?" His arm outstretched, he guides Nolan into an adjacent corridor.

A few doors down, Nolan stops again. He peers through another glass panel situated in another black door.

Inside the room are about a dozen men and women staring into table-top screens. Nolan can see their lips moving in seemingly random patterns. Some are nodding, others frowning, smiling, laughing, crying. None of the room's inhabitants seem the slightest bit aware of those around them. They never take their eyes from the screens.

Nolan cannot help but think of Jenny.

"Find something else of interest?" asks Harshaw.

"What's the theoretical benefit of this charade?"

"It is a failing of character to disregard everything on impulse."

"Not everything, just most things I see going on down here."

"You don't appreciate the larger purpose, Agent Nolan, that's your problem."

"So what's the larger purpose to this?" Nolan turns back to the glass panel in the door.

"You see those screens."

"Yes. Of course I see them."

"What do you see in them?"

"I can't see very clearly from here." Nolan presses his face flat to the glass. "Silhouettes? Heads of some kind?"

"Yes. They see a face, a neck, a pair of shoulders, but what's interesting is what they think they see."

"That one: a Laurel and Hardy film. That one: someone having their brains siphoned out of their heads through a straw. That one…"

"No you misunderstand me. They see a face, but they mistake just whose face it is."

"They think it's theirs. They think it's a reflection."

"They think it's their reflection, yes. They think they are looking into mirrors."

"So what are they doing?"

"They're mimicking their reflections. They are doing what it makes most sense to do, given what they think they know about the image in front of them."

"So you have yourself a consummate little parlour trick. So what? Why keep them there like that?"

"Much as I think you'd benefit from it, I can't be made responsible for your education, Agent Nolan."

"The usual evasive bullshit."

"In many ways, and one very fundamental way, they are no different from the rest of us."

"Which is?"

Harshaw looks away, considering his response. He goes to say something and stops. Eventually, he turns to face Nolan and says, "The only way we become ourselves is by becoming something else."

"And you need them to paint the picture."

Accepting that Nolan is never going to be a sympathetic ear, Harshaw starts off down the corridor. "We should move on. I trust you have other duties to fulfil today."

Nolan follows him.

"The room we want is just down here. When we get there I'll leave you to make your own assessment. Just switch on the monitor and the reason for your presence will become apparent soon enough."

"Why not just tell me?"

"This you need to see."

"You're still to convince me of the necessity of seeing."

"Here we are. I'll be here when you finish."

Nolan enters the room and sits down in front of the monitor. He switches it on and the world around him slides away...

Smell of rotting teeth. Warm wet air falling on his face. Mouth open tasting words.

Nolan opens his eyes, his blood bloating like a corpse.

"…They use information on me. Just another writhing test-subject bleeding from the ears. Blood. You see? I see disambiguation as ice melting. I have an electric kettle and a single electric ring. I'll let you use them, you talk to me nice. My kitchen is a rotting hovel. And small, my kitchen is small. It's just an area, a part of my one room. They say an increase in the disgregation of my molecules means I am unable to go to work today. I need to stay here and see and formalize my ideas. The history of origins began without me. It will not end that way. I won't stand by for that. Do you hear me?"

Nolan turns his head away, his fingers quivering, tinkling the keys on some invisible piano.

"I hear you," Nolan replies, finding the articulation of those three words a struggle.

He looks at the floor, follows it to a wall coloured like a tea stain. The entire floor is clumsily paved with flayed cans, each disassembled can nailed into place by its four corners. Seated, back resting against a metal-framed bed is a half-naked woman, her black hair fanned across the horse-hair mattress, her eyes sewn shut, her belly ripped open spewing intestines like bunched snakes of newborn rodents.

"You like my tin floor? Be fucked without it. They'll come up between the boards all day long you give em the chance. Tongue takes some working here don't it? You'll feel the words again soon enough."

He catches Nolan looking at the dead woman propped up against the bed. "Her legs relaxed after an hour or so, uncoiled my lust all over her. Up for days I was." He pauses, breathing heavily through his nose, as if the stench of her decomposition acted as an aide memoire. In an instant his face begins to twist from the bottom up, his eyes whipped into fog, combed free of objects. "They speak of the motivations of dreams, weak bloods, their heads on the tilt. Hours, days dead through neglect. All those squeamish ideals consigned to icy heavens. Endless life-times spent bound homeward from the sun. My mind's iron mills cut from bite-sized chunks of blank moonlight. I remember before this place a forest marked with paper crosses. I remember my father and his work buddies singing drinking songs to the corpses laid out on the road. I have all my pretties pee as they dance their ragged retreat, their night-bruises thinning in the blue shade, overreached strands of dim pain dancing under the skin like the bleeds in cheap marble. I make my art and my art makes me."

Nolan makes an effort to get up from the floor. He manages to negotiate himself into a sitting position. The room and the view from the window get inside him: hundreds of slimy cigarette ends thick across the tables and spilling from the sink; the air smells like mutton rotting in the sun. There are tiny spots of glossy blood seeping through the bend in the crank's sleeve. A litany of tower blocks obtrudes from blank stretches of industrial hoarding.

"You hear that?" the crank asks.

"I hear a lot of things."

"Unmistakable once you know. Listen! No?"

Nolan shakes his head.

"Clack! Clack! It's a fresh set of heels clattering in the noose. Listen careful and you can hear the pipe creak under the weight."

"I don't hear it."

"No matter. You'll pick it up."

Nolan gets to his feet and sits down on a metal chair. He sees something on the table surrounded by dog ends that takes his interest. He starts to laugh.

"My saucer amuses you?"

"Mother-of-pearl, here! My god-fearing granny loved the stuff, buttons, compacts, picture frames…"

"You think I don't fear God? I fear God. My entire life is an act of worship."

"That's not a god I want to meet."

"Fingernails."

"Huh?"

"The mother-of-pearl: it's fingernails."

"That makes more sense."

Across the stairwell outside two grey-skinned men serenade

a recessed window from their trashcan perches. They watch enraptured as a series of pale faces fade in and out of view like smears on glass.

"They'll never get in there. Better off making do with what's out in the open."

"That what you do?" says Nolan flicking his eyes in the direction of the dead woman.

"My brothers and I stand like ancient columns leaning against the breeze. We keep busy or we fall." The words were polished, and he seemed half-fearful of using them: a snake repackaged as a man feebly embarrassed by his divided tongue.

"What and where is this place?"

"It's pretty much the same as every other place I've ever been, only you need to be careful. Things aren't always... aren't always evident: for example, most of the time I can't tell Kuppfer Men from their victims."

"Kuppfer Men?"

"Assassins. Pleasureless killers. No joy in em, not a drop. Cold fuckers."

"Where? Where are we? You have a geographic location for this place?"

"Not sure it has one. If it has, it might as well not have. We're walled in. It's a trap."

Nolan reaches round to his shoulder holster and finds it empty. "What do you have in the way of protection?" he asks.

"The usual."

"Plus my Govt. issue."

The crank's black eyes are wide, his rank breath heavy. A noise outside the window swipes his attention. Shadows pass across the far wall. He ducks. He places his pale Pterodactyloid fingers over his knees, and holds his position.

"I'm going to need it back," says Nolan, losing patience.

Rising up off his haunches he goes to speak, but Nolan's fist slams into his throat before he can get a syllable out. He falls backwards, gasping for air, his hands at his throat.

"I'm going to need it back."

Unable to speak, he points to the woman and then points to his own stomach.

Nolan reaches inside her and retrieves his gun. "That you bagged it beforehand has saved your life. Thanks for the hospitality."

Nolan walks out into a hallway made fuzzy with failing light and condensation. As he heads down a stairwell he hears the squelch of receding antennae, screams and voices from above and below. There is a sense of timelessness, as if he is locked in some sprawling present running on empty, lost in its own noise like a pluvious night sky.

There are twitching bodies everywhere: unconscious men and women finding spikes in the dough of their dreams. He steps over them, trying to ignore the smell and their garbled noise.

He walks on without direction, but the malign scenery remains constant: old men sit chewing on their cheeks in sealed doorways, on the landings rotating shoals of skinny shadows chanting, light fishbone footsteps of skipping souls, dead arms protruding from brickwork and bin bags, icy smiles hatching tigers, gaffer-taped mouths wrists and ankles, queues of painted corpses with B-movie sensibilities posing for their cigarette moment, smell of backed-up bodies, high-rise windows melting in the sun, men and women faded into action, their movements frantic and un-owned, shrunken, shaded things, the engine of their will torn into a tender sail.

A miserable cloak of un-scrolled faces.

He hears a buzz saw screaming on the floor below.

He follows the noise to a woman cowering in an apartment hallway, puke-tinged skin punctuated with red welts. In the kitchen he finds two men, their protruding stomachs tight against their shirts, searching through frozen limbs packed in polythene bags – forearms, knees and sections of thigh.

They both turn round, and as if immediately identifying him as someone safe to ignore do just that.

One of the men – his eyes domed in clear Perspex, his fat neck a mass of scar tissue – picks up a transparent food processor from a bloodstained worktop. "This ain't chicken."

The other man – the weightier of the two, sporting a nose the tip of which droops down past his lips to his chin – lifts up a scorched cooking dish: "And this char ain't chicken brain."

In another pot is a human head, half of which is boiled into something resembling dog food.

Tall, brawny, gloomy, and bearded, he wanders in mock-gnawing on a section of human spine. "It's a fucking mess in there: gored them all to shit with a blunt chisel. Got his own psychosexual abattoir going on – fucking glass-eyed freak."

He glances over at Nolan, and as if coming to the same conclusion as his friends looks immediately away.

"Time rips through them like salt through a slug, so they avoid it; and this is what they avoid it with." He turns back to Nolan, coaxing a response.

"Who's they?" Nolan asks.

"This one…" he pauses, drumming his thick brown fingers on an empty cigarette packet, "he picks women off the higher-level thoroughfares: the ones with meat on them. Scrawny nerve-fucked babblers ain't his thing. The usual ex-army psychopath developed a taste for sexualizing death; one more shit-heel loner customizing his grot-hole into a feeding ground. The creatures are in there, hanging from home-machined ceiling hooks. By the looks of it he stripped the flex from a whole bunch of kettle leads and put the live wires into their old wounds…"

"You want anything?" says one of the others on his way out the door.

"Taco and black coffee," he says and turns back to Nolan. "There's twenty or more in there, all wrapped in cellophane and missing their limbs, a hundred or so bagged teeth, piles of skin and shelved heads. Execution's clumsy, no real surgical technique to speak of…" He hears a noise coming from a large ground-level kitchen cupboard. He opens it up and pulls a woman out by her hair. Her age is hard to determine. The skin on her arms looks young, mid-twenties at most, but her hair is balding and her teeth are a deep orange. Her face is drawn and mottled with sores. He pulls her up onto her knees. She spits down his legs. He pulls a knife from the worktop block and pushes it into her throat.

Nolan sneers.

The other women looking in from the hallway sit horror-stuffed.

"Potential victim or not, she's the same dirt as the guy who put her there – most of them are."

"And you?"

"Police. Same as you, right?"

"Our methods differ."

"We have only one method here."

"I caught the demonstration."

"Name's Alton."

"Nolan."

"Well, Nolan, all this bug-eyed shit are good for is wiggling and squirming all over each other; fucking and mutilating is all they know. Their minds are gone, every one of them strung out on Belt Candy carving its symbols into everything they come across. I found one of mine this morning: butchered, virtually ripped apart, tri-bar in lipstick on his left breast. They'd opened his neck while he was running a search; head left hanging by a thread. Lines of this shit sodomising him over and over for nigh on a week."

"This place is almost too bad to be true."

"None of these cunts understands truth. They've a thousand fucking channels to block it out, video games, movies, movies, porn…"

"Doesn't sound so different."

"In some ways, no. It's our own Kowloon WC stripped of sweets and smiles and harmony. You want, I'll give you a taste."

Nolan shrugs.

"Follow me!"

He walks out of the room, down the hallway and into another room. The floor is damp. Nolan imagines it as the collective sweat of the soon-to-be-dead. The walls are covered in posters: there are pictures of thin-armed, pert-breasted, cartoon cyberwhores clad in duct tape with hammers in their heads and guns between their legs alongside a selection of Disney and Pokémon characters.

"Take a seat."

Nolan sits in one of two leather armchairs facing toward a huge TV screen.

"Now watch!" says Alton, working the remote.

An undernourished man wearing nothing but a pair of dark blue tracksuit bottoms, his arms and torso heavily tattooed, talks into the camera. Unable to sit still, his knees bouncing continuously, his head and eyes rocking ever so slightly from side to side. Somebody off-screen asks him to relay the activities of the previous night.

"We fucked her into next week. No exaggeration. Fucking whore left her kiddies to starve. Locked them in like dogs with food and water. Enough for a couple of days, she said. Nine days before she got back to them. We all knew. We even joked about it while we were doing her. We'd be tearing up her shitter and laughing about how her kids were probably chewing through the walls by now, how they'd be dead in a few hours. She seemed to get off on it. She laughed along. She howled like a rabid wolf. Three days in and she tried to leave. Her clothes were on and the bolts were off, when Dr O turns up with a couple of 8-Balls. She was going. I really think she was. The timing was beautiful. We were ecstatic, couldn't fucking believe our luck. Watching him dance the tweak right under her snotty nose was too much. We were ruined for hysterics. He slipped his hand between her legs and pushed his burnt fingers inside her. Her eyes turned to glass. She watched the bag come our way. We stopped laughing. Dr O had her prone at our feet. The mother died before her kids. I saw it happen – in that moment. Apparently, that's the way it's supposed to be."

"Sounds like one to remember," says the off-screen female voice.

"Fucking right!" he replies.

Another man appears. He sits in what looks like the same

room on the same chair. He has a thin, patchy beard and licks his lips whenever he pauses for breath.

"Her elimination was visionary: a multi-layered, multi-dimensional dismemberment; some fragments were said to have found their way into the sun."

"The sun?" says the same off-screen voice.

"There's always a paucity of case studies, no paradigm or clinical analysis, only verbal accounts, trial transcripts, hyperbolic data insertions and peripheral academic texts. The environment dictates to a large degree what is left. But I can provide the geographic location of every one of my bite marks. Can you?"

"You've got me there."

"I want to encourage all viewers to join the Hollow Belt Hermeneutic Program today. Let's unite our discoveries..."

He goes on to talk, at considerable length, of inaccessible memories, of sun-drenched excursions lit by a thousand buried light bulbs, defensive structures, aesthetic myths, malfunctioning spectators/phantasms in some page-less dream-text, ecstasies of detail cross-referenced with encyclopedic fervour, with precise indexing and classification. He holds up a photograph of a row of old men staring into paintings of defaced people strolling beneath an apron of declorophyled leaves.

Alton starts scrolling through the channels. "Fucking morons. Ghosts. Everything makes some twisted sense to them. Every day another ingenious project scrawled across another body, their minds decaying in an endless circle of fucked-up fakery.

"Here's one. This guy's finished now. Did for him a week back."

The camera closes in on a set of lips, thread-thin and colourless.

"…from controlled medicines found in Lot 10 back in the Midwest. The Blight and The King of Tears threatened the trade of pseudoepedrine; couldn't have a million over-functioning super-beings morphing with their medicines, burning villainous and unimpeded, now could they. Spent a year importing insects from the Subtle Realms to dig in: manufacturing the wait, in for the drug, the wild cells – synthesized doom-makers on the roadsides of our blind present. The technical work goes on into the never-ending night, tweak-candy demanding its hallucinations, history smoked into a distant fatigue. Rapid states of inflation in our neurotoxic receptors. We take on The Thirst and build Hollywood veneers around his browning stench. Sexual slips of body enforcement in sick air of decongestants and fertilizer, fighting through the 7-11 carcasses in blown labs of nervous respiration everywhere. Their remains watch the blood run at a cold price."

He returns to his rock can bent and black like a slaughterhouse step. His face goes into temporary stasis, head rocking slightly. After a couple of minutes soaking the hit he resumes.

"Anxiety comes from downtime, from succumbing to sleep and having the dawning soil your spirit in some deadly evening hour, your glorious havoc sucked into your four walls, your euphoric skin pale and beleaguered with sores under the false microscope of need, your love cannibalized into a mess of crucified bodies. That there is life disassembling your blank soul, hiding the reality of its dose in low-definition colours and the heavy weight of your so-called absence, is... This is the sequence behind the yellowed, time-sucked skin of self-opposed users. The only remedy is purity of purpose, resilience in high trafficking of time-doses and fall days whose examples of immediacy are fully exploited as items of trade. Our regulators supply cannibalized figures drawn long on wholesale price. Mood medicines, like Yaba love and real people, are conceptual products bent as crash metal. We put them down like a fucking Pfizer slave."

"So to sum up, would you say that your chronically depersonalized, paraphilic indulgences act like the mutating megaspores of some hyper-urbanized distraction, and that..."

Channel change.

A naked man moves in on his homemade bride. Her crudely constructed exoskeleton of metal piping wrapped in pink duct-tape lays sprawled on the floor, legs spread to reveal a huge mutilated rat, legs and tail amputated, eyes stabbed out, mouth cleared of teeth. Bound to the makeshift coccyx with copper wiring, it palpitates like a furry heart. He moves down for the munch, snaking his tongue down the rat's throat – the threat of things to come, foreplay. His face, made up with colouring pens, is reflected in hers, a hand-mirror rammed into the top of her spinal column, lengths of red and white flex glued to its plastic frame. He kisses her lips, pressing down hard, their tongues locked in harmonious struggle: a defeated echo wrestling against itself. He shifts his weight onto one arm and teases her pussy a while with the head of his heavily-veined cock. Soon tiring of the niceties, he rams it home, straight through into those squirming contours (ribbed for his pleasure), displacing blood and organs with every stroke. Having fucked the rat dry he begins sobbing, his tears forming multicoloured pools on her bevel-edged cheek-bones.

Freeze-frame.

Voice-over: "Such are the maggot-marrowed bones of lust; such are the trappings of love."

Channel change: long-haired sack of bone in blood-stained jeans and checkered shirt unbuttoned all the way to the waist.

"Glassies on the border of unwatched time."

He watches a blowfly burn out on the glass, biting at the hardened beds of his missing fingernails.

"Those gin-girls, he reads their vertebrae like Braille."

"Who does?" asks another voice which might as well be the same voice.

"Snap Trap patrols these tunnels, sniffing out tremors in the porn dens, turning hallucinations up for feeding. Sell human tissue strong now..."

Sound of frantic gamers curling through the ventilation shafts, a thousand varieties of squeal, squelch of liberated spines like Wellington boots pulled free of mud.

Yet another lonely man yanking solidarity through a quaking hole in his groin, he jokes about decline, some dry bitch with never-ending legs and video teeth, predators buried in alien gameplay, a lost project born in a concrete bath, whorehouse acrimony running through all them bitches' dirty veins.

Channel change.

"There were mice curled up like socks inside his mouth and scorpions nesting in what was left of his brain, and being slow on the uptake we still call that death, don't have much time for the new names, I mean I'm supposed to spot this shit in here and what woman don't got Benign Ovarian Voices?" Her raked right arm swings round identifying her tangled brood in various stages of affliction, acne bubbling under the skin where it can't be got at. "Best to forget about how truth once had a smell."

And the voice is gone and it takes her a while to notice. The boy beside her pitches in: "Her tongue's a parasite and feeding now so there won't be no noise there for a while…. Yeah on the softs of her mouth, not much left but it ain't greedy, takes its time, waits for the healing to happen, but she's spinning you on the not knowing. She got all the alienages in that dented up head o hers, all the auto-voyeurisms, the phantom haemophilias, the partial-body nihilisms, cupboard dementias, croc mouth, the vascular gonorrhoea, genital dystrophy, black river dementia, projected psoriasis, diarrheal narcolepsy, legionhead syndromes, converse hypertrophies, varicose pregnancies, adrenalized comas, the gamut and more and she can diagnose at a glance, and cold with a spade too, but her eyes like old church windows bathe this shit in God's light coloured in reds and greens and gold. It's like we was just words in some new language, some monster slang coined with some precision we can't get coz we're smeared across it and maybe it's not got more than one thing to say, one sentence made of rooms, of all them windows wearing necks, them backbones coiled like sleeping snakes, of embryos raped with abstract forms of fossilized babies, of wolfmen their howling brains written in spiders, of men tempted from their skins with the smell of a tribe, or maybe all this is gonna create some new world and we're being remade to fit, but it's better here than where I was; can't move for the godsick back there, dead children refusing to be forgotten still growing inside their mothers, and least you boys got names for the stuff what's missing even if you're tongue-cut on the new shit."

He looks round him at the children. "I think this one ere's my brother," he says.

"You don't know?" says the off-screen voice.

He scratches at his groin and smiles at the woman. "Might need to do some calculations before I can answer that."

The woman tries to speak but nothing comes out.

Channel change.

"Fire the bowl, bitch! Fire in the Bowl! Fire in the Bowl!" The household chant from five gamers pressed into sofas, heartbeats cut from a hunting cheetah.

They each talk in turn.

"Some doom missions happen in the dark, some under the full blaze of halogen. There are gameworld payoffs: we can mould their faces in whatever configurations we desire; we can tweak features, sex, and voices depending on genre, build and kill everything that moves. Protagonists of barbaric magnitude, my friend."

"And what about precautions to ensure survival?" says the off-screen voice.

"I don't bother with cover mechanics, if that's what you mean: fucking shit's for pussies."

"Fuck off!" the others roar in unison.

"Exaggerated physics allows us to tear up normal human beings as if they're made of paper. We can drain their life bars in concentrated bursts of slow-mo co-op torture. Always looking to redefine the tired blur of deathmatch modes."

A wall of third-person perspectives closes in on her as she tosses her lank tresses with cinematic flair. Suffocating atmosphere as someone named Earl levels the game, dispatching some clean prey with a dose of "crude stealth mechanics".

Someone mentions a nocturnal button-mashing incident involving a nailgun's auto-aim feature, and light-hearted bickering ensues.

They all pause to recover health by firing up their bowls.

"We become virtually invisible if we stand in one another's shadows. We have context-sensitive onscreen icons – see there? They point out when you can use an implement for orifice creation, skin a face without tempering sex drive, hoist a body up for display, et cetera. You can learn to identify the dark you can hide in at a glance…"

"Toilets and bathrooms are littered with single-use weapons like bottles and plastic bags."

"At default speed none of us can relax or stay prone: our settings won't allow it."

"Instant-kill moves are frowned upon round these parts. Right, boys?"

They all concur enthusiastically.

"I see everything in video filter mode; it's all one great big fucking lunatic exhibit."

"Some of the challenge can start to feel rather artificial, grainy, everyone wearing a washed-out look of dead flesh, little more than window-dressing in a butcher's shop."

"Better not be directed at me, pal. You wanna catch your reflection sometime."

"Our life is carefully contrived."

Only one bone-bent illuminato manages to spy The Hook Man pass by the door with his attaché case.

He's immobilized in seconds.

Blood spurts all over the camera lens.

The view is cleared with a piece of cloth.

"Inside you'll see hanged bodies, which respond realistically if pushed. But the limited range of audio effects can start to seem a little phony; no less, the sound of your own heart beating. Also, there are slight frame-rate drops on occasion."

Three green arrows circle her blistered mouth, her anus

gulping air like a fish in a bucket.

"As the brain splatters dry on your clothes the fusion meter will hit its peak."

"Inexperienced players sometimes behave very unrealistically, like some mysterious agency keeps switching them back to default behind-the-back perspective." He takes centre and gets busy, toiling at the room's flab in a boosted daze.

Voice Over: "Since self-preservation doesn't seem important to them, deaths can appear unworldly and inconsequential. The crowds outside are mostly for decoration. They work best from a distance. Try to interact and the sphex-glitches show themselves. They're best left alone. They play nameless, voiceless, re-imagined versions of themselves, the storyline as ineffectual as their identities."

Smell of stale sex rising from dead bodies in spaghetti waves.

"Would you agree that however much one augments the human experience, there are still times when existence appears to be nothing but a tired collection of cut scenes?" says the off-screen voice.

"That's something you have to fight against."

They are unanimous on this.

"You appear to tune in on any logic breaches and make them your own."

"Assimilate! Assimilate!"

"Always be assimilating."

Monotonous screams, tinny and subdued, emit from the

corner of the room.

Quicksave progress in dank corridor crawling with new combatants, their orange eyes glowing up, their leprose hands breaking up, movement prone to time-lag.

"The player sees through my eyes for the full duration of each chapter," says one of the gamers looking up from the floor.

Two of them surrounded by a maze of headcrab zombies in trademark crowbar melee combat scene.

"Los Ganados! Los Ganados!"

Voice Over: "We found a body hanging in their closet: the result of yesterday's session. She had been strangled, raped and sodomized with a crowbar, her face completely decimated with the same weapon."

"We all saw the puncture marks of Crucifer in her neck. What, we're supposed to just leave her be?"

Someone had taken a carving knife to her thighs, hacking out ten circles of flesh in the grey light.

"Where's the guy with the blue hair that was here last week?" says the off-screen voice.

"He left."

"Yeah, he went a few days ago."

"No he was here yesterday."

"No he wasn't."

"I saw him today."

"I heard The Plumber talking to him an hour ago."

They find him in the next room, his own genitals tied around his neck, his cheekbones crushed, his femur fractured, his remains repeatedly brutalized, live bugs in the pantyhose used to asphyxiate him. Around his body are blunt instruments covered in his brain tissue; there are footprints up the walls, and semen seeping from his open wounds; his anus has been assaulted with a broken ketchup bottle, his skull caved in and a portion of his brain exposed. Most of his teeth are found in a jam jar placed on a stack of turn-of-the-century mug shots.

"You seen enough?" says Alton, turning to Nolan.

Voice Over: "Passengers in their own heads watching their watching in a multi-dimensional haze of constantly re-imagined instruments…"

"Yeah, I'm done."

"Ready for the real thing now, eh?" he gets to his feet. "Well, you coming?"

"Where to?"

"We're heading for The Floor: the ground-level. Might as well tag along, less you got someplace else to be."

"Not in here I don't."

Nolan follows Alton into the hallway, where his men have already executed the remaining victims. (The one from the kitchen blooded the black street fourteen floors down.) They both stand outside eating and drinking. One of them hands a Styrofoam cup and a greasy paper bag to Alton, who leads the way down the stairwell.

Dreams of Amputation

Down on The Floor Nolan gets a running commentary on his surroundings. In whichever direction he looks, one of the three is ready with some background.

Nolan watches slug-type men nestling into sweaty refuse sacks in flux with thousands of wrestling maggots.

"Amputees. Alcoholics, most of them, subject to blackouts and fits of decorporealisation. They crawl inside there for warmth."

"Warmth? I'm in the middle of a fucking flame down here."

"Tell them that," says Alton, allowing himself a smile.

Everywhere bodies are battered soggy, in windows teeth collected in paper cups. In the faces of those they pass, staring up from the wet ground, is a spun-eyed claustrophobia brought about by their over-scrutinized surroundings, dark and dank, the milieu of an abandoned asylum, its decrepit roof allowing the warm rain to tap at your skull like a cavity nester, the sun torn into a thousand strands of dampened gloom. Grimy old whores peddling their wizened clams, slick with butter, to the ghosts drifting in and out of strip joints and pornographic cinemas.

Numerous amputees sit in doorways humming and stroking their withered stumps. "What's with the hack jobs?" asks Nolan.

"Deciphering tingles. Mad fucks think they receive messages and premonitions from their missing limbs." Alton laughs.

"Ever hear any of them?"

"Heard plenty. All of them bullshit."

Like flies trailing misfortune and shit they move through the shifting streets, grimy and repetitive, sparks of congregated sorrow fizzing in the damp air. A dog, long dead, melts into the slimy right angle where wall meets floor. Men dyed orange interact with corpses, animating them, French kissing their Taco mouths. Fly-blown torsos surface in the quad's statue-lined cesspools. Forward, weaving patterns of slumped despair from rattled insomniacs imagining themselves preened and munificent in glass confusion.

Most of the inhabitants still wear human clothes, but the incongruity soon becomes apparent.

"'Ergonomic maximization of captive mechanisms help condition the inhabitants to the authoritarian logos of an impossibly stretched present.' That's the official line."

Deep cracks shadow movement in their deepest regions, and an amorphous maze of wires and pipes creeps down the walls like exo-veins. Heavy voices cascading down through to The Floor, thrumming in the ears like some continuous and far-flung colostomy belch. Tomorrows pass into the sick earth of a neglected and carnivorous past.

"So what's it like up top?" asks Nolan.

"From here to the Balconies right up to the Metal Forest, the differences are immaterial to us," says the trunked Police, eager to reply. "We ain't the guys to ask."

"The distractions are brighter, more pervasive," says Alton.

"Everything seems less desperate, but it isn't: it's the same shit."

Nolan hears the lame grinding of porn theatres. Rows of curled-up men ragging their stumps to looping torture flicks, Hollywood sweethearts advancing in measured paces from the couch to the noose. Collective sound of sun-starved women clad in haunted dresses swallowing their screams. Men caged in their own shadows digging through an inventory of asphyxiated emotions.

"The old flick and stick," says the dome-eyed Police. "It's timeless."

Through an open door Nolan stands watching a party of fleshy metronomes. The puzzled detail of their faces belies the smooth, patterned order of their encounter. A vagina breaks free of its repeated union, pulsating grotesquely like a garroted throat. There are joints in her laughter where some damaged humanity might have resided if there'd been a poet present to give it dignity; instead the silent seams are filled with snorts, the sliding of nooses, and electrodes sucking on loose skin. He watches a man finger the grey dough of her gut, his damaged gaze made up of old fragments of a distant explosion. An unowned smile creeps up her cheeks.

Alton comes up alongside him. "They're in a loop. They'll be there for days. They'll be there till there's nothing left."

Nolan wanders off from the group into a room lined in what look like pigeon feathers. In the middle of the floor sits a man nursing his mate. Hearing Nolan enter, he looks up.

"Some say it's like waking up," says the man in earnest, "but it ain't. Unless you remember what it's like to wake up as a young child, and you don't. When they wake up – them outside, doe-eyed sleepwalkers every one – they just exchange one sleep for another."

His fingers strum her sticky hair. Smell of used-up orifices left to the flies. Carbonated blood dancing in her gullet, and crucifixes cut into her fingerless hands. Preserved yawns doubling up as ashtrays, urinals. Dirty fingers in the pie with faces up on leave from hell. Nolan can see the fear of heaven in their black eyes, for this workshop of appetites is pitiless and eternal.

Alongside the man's week-old supper is some kind of asemic code assembled from veins. Nolan can't take his eyes off it.

"It came out that way. I didn't alter the arrangement one bit. It efforts me to even contemplate it. And to think all his dreams came crystal-laced in Honolulu."

Doubtful, Nolan says, "How did you get it out without damaging it?"

"Look, we are the ones occupied, focused, more than alive. We find tedium and we burn like vampires in the sun. I don't believe in the birds that greet the morning. Bring me The Plumber!"

Nolan turns, making to leave.

"Why do you have a face like a screwed up photo?" the man asks, with the naive curiosity of a child.

Alton eases by Nolan and shoots the man in the head. "Rude

cunt. Come on, let's go."

Every now and then one of Alton's men pulls a gored face up from a puddle of dirty rain, and then kicks the body over onto its back.

"Some of these fuckers'll do anything for some shut-eye," says Alton, sensing Nolan's curiosity. "We've found tweakers hiding out in hollowed-out bodies just to get some peace and quiet. Screams from the waste disposal is the first we know of them. Seen them stirring up dust after being dormant a full month."

Molluscan torsos slime up the ground-floor walkways, their toxic mucus coating walls and ceilings, eating through electrical cable as they wend through the pillared central courtyard, sacks sweating maggots, cigarettes burning anomalous patterns. Piles of Floor citizens lie clucking in the shadows, their thin faces peeling away like damp wallpaper.

They move into and out of a series of towers, ascending gradually through numerous stairwells.

"Through here!" Alton gestures to a narrow-gutted, arched alleyway. Nolan follows them through.

At the end it opens up into an expansive but low-ceilinged enclosure. Down one wall a row of tall men in white overalls stoop over benches clouded in abnormally dense vapours, their dry tongues trawling sialoid ash about their mouths like slugs in the sun, an archived neglect turning toxic just beneath the skin.

"These Plastic Men," Alton explains, "cook only for their

official neurotransmitter, some kind of metastatic Garguax promising to deliver them to new worlds."

"This lab's crawling with new glassware," says the trunked Police.

"I see it," says Alton. He turns to Nolan. "There was an explosion here yesterday."

Nolan scans the room. The red coral aftermath of the recent fulmination still decorates most surfaces: fragments of cartilage and bone are sprayed across the ceiling's sunset like impulsive stars. Countless dismembered newborn limbs twitch and shift like alien life-forms desperate for the cover of shadow. One of yesterday's cooks – CNS raging like a Los Angeles freeway – is still waltzing his intestines around the room, his eyes crystal ruins, subjectless, glossy conglomerations of endless moments; he recites mangled recipes as he goes: "Dextropolamine 22-B aka Egyptian Meth kitty litter blues (sodium silicate) hydrogen peroxide, iodine tincture, Epson salt (Magnesium sulfate)... anhydrous ammonia (fertilizer gold), red phosphorus (matchbox strike), lithium (batteries)..."

The 22s line the worktops, their blood-like contents (pseudoephedrine, red phosphorus and hydriodic acid) spuming in unison. Orange hoses unfurl like tentacles from the neck, running reaction gases to rows of cat litter trays.

Directed at some imagined audience, one of the cooks shouts, "See that, you jelly jar motherfuckers? That's industry!"

A sea of Sudafed bottles in the stairwell, dead bodies bobbing like kids in a ball pool, but Nolan's eyes are still polluted with the greasy flesh up on that caged balcony bathed in sunlight, those limp shadow-diced bodies kissing the floor, entire districts of their brains masticated by imaginary timelines.

A pair of blood-soaked high heels swing from overhead wiring as he enters the room.

"Shit! If it ain't The Plumber… Come in! Come in!"

A voice from another room: "Someone get him to take a look at the drains!"

A man gets to his feet. "Tssk,tssk. I don't like the look of this. This pipe-work's aggressive, straight from Freddy's basement, fucking burning hot, take the skin off your arm…" he collapses back in his armchair, laughing maniacally.

The plumber leans against the wall and whistles with a sophistication and precision worthy of Fred Lowery himself, the back pocket of his overalls waving the undigested fantasies of the day as he saunters from room to room, his frown a rooted parasite draining all stray endorphins from his brain.

Blistered hysterics crawl through the plumber's labyrinthine indulgences, plotlines crimped and brazed into gurgling exhibits of emancipation, its tangles impenetrable, implausible visualizations of some ragged model of amputation manufactured in the dark. He wears the remote skin of the perpetual onlooker, the recording device consumed by the processes of consumption. He experiments with new materials: high-pressure pumps and plastic pipes that twist and flex like boneless limbs, ornamental valves, elbows and unions fashioned from recycled gastro tract, and hyper-sensitive recording equipment attuned to the sound of leaks.

Naked bodies chiseled with distraction lounge along the walls, their hair alive: stone faced Hydras woken to the slump mirror. Some fragments fall from the plumber's pockets. They shake their heads as they watch the scraps of paper flutter to the ground. A bloated silence as the plumber's eyes trawl the un-bagged specimens. He gently gathers up the contraband as if they were little paper animations of hope, tiny harvested micro-states of jelly-headed want.

Figures bound in cable hiss through rotten teeth, intoxi-cated by the thud of his work-boots they writhe and spit and whimper like wired fish.

The rain pouring in through the roof sounds like applause as they make their way along the top floor of a block Alton refers to as "Plato Flats," its farmed sunlight cutting them into strips. Bursts of random laughter followed them all the way up and continue still; it's as if the place is consumed by its own personal joke.

Nolan's feet kick through paper bindles, ankle deep in places. He thinks back on the journey up: bloodshed of ten or more scattered morning suns.

"It's a kind of living death they lead in here: a perpetual narcolepsy of the soul," Alton says as he watches the rain fire in through the broken windows and smash off the sill.

"Most of them seem alive enough to me," says Nolan.

"Yeah, but you need to ask yourself about the where, and more importantly the when of that life."

"I don't follow."

"Look, one hit into the glass and they're lost for a second time, and for good."

"A second time?"

"Let's pay Abattoir a visit. You'll see. Like the lab guys, he's one we tend to leave alone – for now, at least."

"Why?"

"He's displaying uncommon resilience. But he'll go the same way as the rest eventually."

"Which is?"

"Into nothing and nowhere, cooked translucent, all the way down to schlong and veneers. But he's not there yet; you'll be able to see the difference."

They come to a door cased in metal. Alton retrieves a key from his pocket, opens the door and leads them in. Before entering the main living area he turns to Nolan: "We keep it tight in here, in view of one another at all times. No use taking any risks."

Nolan nods and follows them in.

The first thing that hits him is the pink light streaming in through the glass doors that run the entire width of the room. Everyone is wearing shades, even the stiffs.

Alton sits down in front of a long-haired man seated in a low armchair in the centre of the room facing the balcony.

"You're blocking my light."

"You asking me to move?" Alton replies.

"For you I'll make an exception."

"There's that famous Abattoir hospitality I've heard so much about."

"Of course. Welcome to my little hive of time-traffickers. Look at them all quaking like a black momma's bucket in honour of your visit."

They talk in hushed tones for a couple of minutes and then Abattoir's voice gets louder and higher, his lungs tightening as he unfolds old tales of Mexico, Honolulu, Arkansas, his feet fidgeting excitedly in a swamp of porno magazines and comics covered in shit and semen.

The reactions of those around him unfurl in a series of still photos. They sit watching cartoons through splashes of fresh blood, the air clinging to the insides of their mouths like cellophane.

"There are all the channels you want in Hell," says the trunked Police standing alongside Nolan, their backs to the wall.

Dreams of Amputation

Rows of eyes like swollen full stops trained on bowls of black glass and slim chambers of white spiraled smoke: FOCUS, focus inside the disorder of stalled lives, lives free of paraphernalia: time without its equipment, thinned time, pure time; the sanguine liquidity of unencumbered duration, of hearts eaten by their beats inside twitching ghosts mincing anxiety into coiling worms of tenseless time.

Atrophic Trailheads roam room to room reciting second-hand memories of times homeless and insomniac in the Midwest: all Abattoir's acolytes end up appropriating his reminiscences as their own.

"Confusions leave me real quick, blurred like faces on a passing train," says Abattoir proudly.

"Carbonated brain tissue fit only for research purposes," Alton counters, "teeth reduced to powder, souls vaporized, ulcers, salted lips, deficit of right-side grey matter, of nerve cells, swollen right-side ventricles, shrunken hippocampus and increased white matter, years arrested in cold delusion, hours spent masturbating into dead containers… None of you can afford to pay the cost of all those crystallized years."

"We bring them in with the salt blocks and EPTs," Abattoir points in the general direction of his entourage, "their mouths already stained with a million bitter breaths. But the physical deterioration of our members is exaggerated. They source their poster children from our rejects – poster boys of oblivion, drones that once scavenged our batteries and then left to inhabit their own vapour trails – peeling open dead mouths to display their oaken teeth rotting into bleeding gums; the antithesis of the Hollywood smile with its glossy porcelains and reinforced jaws."

"You're not selling it to me."

"Give it time. We'll get you speaking Hmong sooner or later."

"Dangerous, those delusions of yours."

"Now finding your thoughts back in Oregon on squeaking swings, that's fucking dangerous. My mother's fingernails chewed all the way down. Constant smell of Marlboros and fertilizer."

"That before you killed her?"

"Could have been. As you know, I took my time." His smile is akin to a disfigurement.

"With all of them, so I hear."

"Wouldn't have felt right to rush." Suddenly he notices someone staggering about by the balcony doors. "Get that hep cunt the fuck out before someone starts raggin its drains!" He turns back to Alton, "And they try to tell you psychosis is odourless."

Alton allows himself to laugh.

Nolan watches as two pairs of hands do for the diseased man's tightly-sprung face. More arrive and do for the rest of him, multiplying on the violence like snake heads on a Hydra. A saw flaps in the air, its teeth clogged with flesh. As they drag him out of the room, Nolan notices that someone has pushed a lit sparkler deep into the man's penis.

Minutes later one of Abattoir's more capable minions calls down two "drones" from the roof, adobe tan on the faces and hands, bodies a pale, part-translucent jelly.

"Dispose of that!" Abattoir shouts at them as soon as they enter.

One at the hands, one at the feet, they drag the body of a woman, skin as smooth and white as a coroner's slab, across the carpet. As they pass Nolan she frees her right arm and grabs his hand. Tiny filaments of an almost robotic trauma arrange themselves across her face. They wrench her away and carry her out onto the stairwell, where they proceed to tip her over the rail. Excited, they watch her descent.

Nolan studies the depressions in his right hand – the hollow marks of terrified fingers refusing to relinquish their grip, despite them now being more than twenty floors down.

The trunked Police leans over to Nolan: "They beat her two-month-old son to death; mistook him for an over-sized rat."

Nolan continues staring at his hand.

Abattoir rummages around in a plastic bag and pulls out some scraps of paper. "We found these the other day," he says, handing them to Alton.

Alton reads from the top of the small pile: "Always beyond even if there isn't one – especially if there isn't one – feeding a worm-life looking to burrow deeper: blind, sexless, endless, doomed..."

"What's with the sudden interest in The Plumber?"

Alton reads from another scrap: "I am the rain: eternal, cursed, ageless, indifferent and falling."

"Quite the enigma, eh?"

"Maybe."

Intoxicated by their own beauty, two women stare into mirrors, teeth grinding out a series of brown smiles, their salivary glands dry as a spinster's twat. Behind them, holding their cuffs, is an old man. He sits nursing his thigh, crystal-dicked, slugging cokes and gorging sugared donuts. His face is pudgy and wan, like a late Goya self-portrait.

A couple of Abattoir's henchmen trawl in some new playthings. A woman, tall and brunette, is at the front of the line.

As Alton gets up to leave, Abattoir goes into his spiel: "Human in my dreams, baby. I swear I'm human in my dreams. Louisiana versions through my green dick – sprayed me far and wide, far and wide... pumped stars into excrement, baby – this here's an endangered species, make you puke your lungs out onta yer chest, darling... don't need no passcode for dem lips, Sweetcheeks."

Behind her a boy, fifteen, no more, straight from his bedroom in Oakton, Va., sweat running down the arms of his black trench coat.

"No agents hiding in the basement here, son. You want I should interview you? Sit your ass down and taste freedom!"

Abattoir takes his thin white hand and pushes it inside a gaping cunt yawning up from the floor. "Now you gonna tell me that's simulation, boy."

"It's a rabbit hole alright…"

"Fuck! I like you, boy. Cut from the same stuff you and me – my cat."

"What's so special about this plumber guy?" Nolan asks, once back outside the apartment in the relative privacy of the hallway.

Alton shrugs. "He's a newcomer. Always taking notes and preaching about the purity of this place and most everyone in it. They reckon him as some kind of messiah."

"Purity?"

"Apparently he reveres their ability to expunge past and future in favour of an endless present. He insists on reminding them of their freedom."

"What does he look like?"

"Nothing out of the ordinary. Blue overalls, average height…"

"Blue overalls!"

As the room gradually comes back to him, Nolan is consumed by ferocious tremors, his limbs curling and jerking, each saltation more violent than the next, like the exhausting serenade of a strychnine poisoning, until finally he slumps back into the seat and eats the air in greedy chunks, sweat pouring out of his neck into his open collar. He remains that way for ten minutes or more before finally attempting to stand.

His legs buckle on route to the door, but he manages to stay upright. The door slides open and Harshaw is there to greet him.

"Now you see my predicament, Agent Nolan."

"Who else… who else knows about this?"

"Please get your breath back, Agent Nolan. Give your brain time to readjust. There's no hurry."

"Who else?"

"I can think of at least one other." Harshaw makes a valiant attempt at forming a smile.

"Apart from that."

"At present, I'd say it was just you and me, but I couldn't be certain."

"You're lying."

"Of course I'm lying, Agent Nolan. Of course I'm lying."

"I want names. I want the source. Where did it come from?"

"Now I think that is something you already know: your consternation, the fact that you're bathed in sweat… You're panicking. Give yourself time. There's no hurry."

"Are you going to cooperate, Harshaw, or…"

"Or?"

"Start talking!"

Harshaw's eyes start flicking from side to side. "Rrrrummaging estimations under the skin… aaaavoid me, get away from… psychotic, our known blackouts scaffold of dreams, human infections, voiceless mass, ideological wash of mankind's remains of men in glass comas of pornography and repetition… system of green passengers, veins siphoning minds into the vacuum… evidence edited into fake histories, a hardened present and a lonely death… their tapestries implement many identities… Hell hidden in a toolbag… you need to find The Plumber… you need to talk to The Plumber… primal amusements, corrupted physics sliced into starved ideals… The Hollow Belt is what's left. At the end, the Hollow Belt is all that's left…"

"Professor! Professor Harshaw!"

"The Plumber moves through the cutting grounds to his lock up.… er, er, er, er…"

"The Plumber's a Sage! I know him. I had him birthed. Who put him in there? Answer me! Who put him in there?"

Nolan goes to touch Harshaw's arm, but pulls back at the last minute. He watches as his eyes roll back and his tongue starts swelling up inside his gaping mouth.

Nolan makes a run for the elevator.

Surprised that his tails have not yet seen fit to intercept him, Nolan wastes no time getting off the street and into 53rd precinct. He runs up the stairs to his division office and goes straight in. As he enters he sees Grice leaning against a desk chewing on his cuff.

"The H-Belt, what do you know about it?" shouts Nolan across the room.

Grice turns around. "Where have you been?" he asks.

"I don't have much time."

"Hadn't we better…" Grice points in the direction of Nolan's office.

Nolan shrugs. "What for?"

"Some privacy," replies Grice, confused.

"Privacy's an illusion; we're a fucking illusion. We can talk here; it makes no difference."

"Are you okay? Have you had another seizure?"

"No. I was in the Tubes. Remember?"

"Of course, I passed you the call."

"I need everything we have on the H-Belt."

"The H6 Quadrant south of the Tubes?"

"No. The Hollow Belt!"

"Where then?"

"I don't know. I don't know where it is."

"What then? What is it?"

"Hard to say. Unappealing."

"You've been there!"

"Yes."

"Then how can you not know where it is?"

"I've no recollection of getting in there or getting out of there, only of being in the Tubes, then being there, and then being back in the Tubes again."

"So it's hidden somewhere in the Tubes then?"

"It was above ground."

"Maybe it just seemed that way."

"I felt the rain."

"Rain feels like any other water, right?"

"Huh," says Nolan, distractedly.

"Look, all I'm saying is that you can't rule out the possibility that you never left the Tubes."

"Who would know? If it was down there, who would know?"

"What did Harshaw say?"

"He found it hard to say anything once his tongue had swollen up to the size of a pillow."

"There's Smithson, I suppose. He trained with Harshaw, and he's made fairly regular visits to the Tubes over the last couple of years. I think he acts as advisor on some of the sick projects they have going on down there. He might know something."

"I'd be surprised if that poisonous toad wasn't birthed in there."

"Well he can't get enough of you."

"How so?"

"He made contact twice last week, asking after you, asking after Jenny."

"And you wait till now to tell me."

"What? This is the first I've seen of you. Nobody could get hold of you. It wasn't as if…"

"You're telling me I've been gone a week?"

"Shy a day, yes."

"I just presumed…"

"The same day… You thought it was the same day?"

"I had no reason to think otherwise."

"So you haven't heard about Sybaris6, and all the other…"

"What about Sybaris6?" asks Nolan, piqued.

"Thursday last week, they all just come to and resume their lives as if nothing's happened, carry on eating their breakfast, dressing for work. Can you imagine it? After all that time. And then Sybaris 2 goes down with it: the exact same scenario."

"What about Spectre Field?"

"They haven't reported any change, but that's not to say… well you know what they're like. We wouldn't be the first to know."

"You said Smithson asked after Jenny. What did he want? Do you think he knows something?"

"I figured he was on a wind-up. Kept mentioning favours, making allusions to debts going unpaid, and then he starts talking about you two, and how he hopes things work out for the best. The man needs to work some on his sincerity."

"He say anything else?"

"No, nothing worth remembering. But the real news is all the minor cases happening worldwide. There've been reports of people the world over slipping in and out of stasis. You don't think you…"

Nolan's face-screens approximate a dyspeptic glare.

"Well the symptoms aren't much different. You can't say where you were."

"I told you where I was; I was in the H-Belt. There were others in there. I wasn't the only person. This ain't some comatose fantasy."

"Shit, I don't know. I'm lost with all this crap; my sister has no time for anything but surveillance now. She doesn't wash; she doesn't talk; she's moved over to dupes; she's in a right state."

"Maybe you should have her put under observation."

"Her and a hundred others, and those are just the reported instances in her sub-district. There's a whole network of them, all swapping reports and fuelling one another's psychosis."

"Look, I know you've got your own shit to deal with, but I need you to say you'll look in on Jenny, watch out for her."

"When?"

"If. That you'll do it if I can't."

"Course I'll do it, but…"

"Last time I was there I added your name to mine. I authorised your access."

"Okay."

Nolan makes to leave.

"You want back-up?"

"No. Stay here and see if you can find out where I've been for the past fucking week."

"And you?"

"Smithson."

She sits slumped in the passenger seat of the car in a lay-by on the edge of the desert. The dunes in the distance twist and glimmer like coils of barbed wire. Her door is open, and her long partially defleshed legs extend free of the car, her heels buried in white ash a metre apart. Her hair is greasy and balding. Her white, strapless summer dress mimics the rhythms of her vermicular throng. The sun scorches her legs while her face remains hidden in the shade. She falls forward, her sunglasses slipping down onto the end of her chewed up nose, and smiles. Her teeth are thin black prongs, warped like burnt matchsticks. Her eyes are missing.

"I warned you," she says.

She places her hands on her kneecaps, and inclines her half-eaten face toward the sun.

"You can't come here anymore," she says; "There's nothing for you here anymore."

She slides her sunglasses back up over her eye sockets, and

disintegrates in the relative cool of the car.

The day Nolan lost contact with the Sage he allowed himself a brief moment of joy, a tiny scrap of untrammelled hope. Even the nagging sense of intrusion between his ears seemed to ease a little to mark the occasion. It happened at precisely 23.52. He'd just finished his circuits round the terrace, and came in to his computer screen flashing the words: 'DIAGNOSTIC RE-PORT: CONNECTION WITH TEST SUBJECT LOST'. On retesting, he found what he'd wanted to find, what he'd been dreaming of for years: the connection completely vanished, the Sage irretrievably missing.

Being this close to his dream made him feel vulnerable. He vowed to move things along as quickly as possible. He planned to run some tests on him the next day, just to be sure.

The visit didn't go as planned. When Nolan arrived, he found the container empty. The screens were still scrolling, but the Sage had gone. There was no way out from the inside, so Nolan knew that someone had to have aided his escape, or most likely extracted him for some purpose forged outside his skull.

The Sage's absence made him nervous, but Nolan decided to gather up any fresh data he could find before leaving. There were a considerable number of reports made in the hours fol-lowing his disconnection, more than he'd expected. Nolan collected them all together and left, waiting till he was a mile or so clear of the container before giving them anything more than a cursory look.

What he found, there on the outskirts of the desert, the sun slowly cooking his right hand through the windscreen, was not the categorical success he'd hoped for. The Sage had survived, but then he hadn't seriously reckoned on death as a likely outcome. He'd harboured other, more well-founded concerns and there were signs of their validity there in those reports: deterioration of memory, marked alteration in personality, acute disorientation, episodes of mania, and possible brain damage.

But that wasn't the end of it, for all of a sudden there was talk of remote comrades locked into the same clandestine struggle as the Sage, in particular a man referred to only as ZS1. Nolan couldn't work out how to interpret this information.

A red notebook lay open in the middle of a pile of reports. Nolan turned it over. On the last used page, beneath some pretty standard script notation was a block of scrawl that regardless of how many times he read it made not the slightest sense.

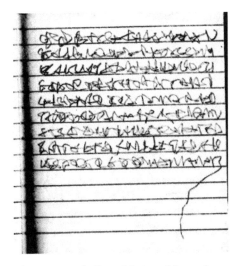

He tore out the page and slipped it into his pocket.

Still unsure as to the safety of the cipher and not expecting a revelation any time soon – its innocuity was still in doubt, and would remain so for as long as it took him to track down the Sage – he put his haul on the seat beside him and started the car.

"Diversion overcomes them, reinforcing its hold second by second, all of them weaned on wishing-well emptiness, all losing their being to The Entertainment Database... Where's the rest of the data we accumulated from Nolan's latest attempt?"

A grey-faced, corkscrewed little clerk sits hunched over a table-top screen. "We're getting it up now, sir."

The Overseer's blue eyes drift over the twitching sea of Spectre8s, their faces doused in watching – stripped of the artistry of forgetfulness, screens disgorging conscripted appearance straight back into the slack earth of their brains. Disbelieving nods left behind in the gutless dreams of open veins, in surfaces without position, and the internal itch of nostalgic diagnoses. "It's quite beautiful. Don't you agree, gentlemen?"

His aides waste no time in expressing their mewling concurrence.

"To think, some people pity them. I envy them. What bliss it must be to be lost in such full engagement, every mental resource tapped to the hilt. No place for the pain of self to intrude. How truly wondrous."

"People don't understand, sir," says his assistant, dutifully standing at his side.

"I could watch them forever."

A couple of metres inside the north perimeter fence of Lab South5 are ten white cubes spaced an equal distance apart. They comprise the living accommodation for the Lab's ten workers. It is considered safer and more productive for lab employees to live on site, and as the cubes are virtually impenetrable without the correct code, the employees are on the whole happy to sacrifice a little of their independence for the reward of such impressive security. Nothing has been done to distinguish one from any of the others: there are no gardens to tend, just fine white gravel, and no homely external adornments to paint or polish.

One cube in from the eastern end is where Smithson resides during his hours of non-service. Barring the odd lascivious excursion and the even more infrequent work-related junket, he remains within the confines of the site, all his day-to-day living needs having been provided by his employer.

It is 13:05 and the sun is a septic lesion on the otherwise grey sky. Smithson is in from the heat and snacking on soft blue cheese and crackers. Sweat bubbles up on his forehead and around his soft pulpy neck.

"No, not a great morning, but the afternoon will be better," he says, grabbing another box of crackers from the drawer.

"So many painstaking details, and... Yes, I know; you're right, and I do appreciate the importance of maintaining the feed; it's just that it's all there in the little stuff, and I can't help... Impudent, yes I see... Do not extrapolate. Do not extrapolate. Okay, I'll make it my mantra, but it's hard not to."

His mouth wide, he inserts a cracker piled high with a hulking slab of cheese.

"I can't resist taunting them... Of course, divulgences suitably opaque unless... Well it doesn't make any difference then... Exactly right."

He lumbers into the lounge area, a trail of soggy crumbs marking his slow transit.

"Well, yes, he's the perfect study case – couldn't have wished for better."

He collapses into a large, luxuriously furnished chair, and sets about arranging his snacks on a tray built into the arm.

"This new lacuna is a perfect replacement. More resilient than the old ones, definitely: its simplicity is exquisite; it has virtually no conversion delay, and its potential manipulation yield is huge."

His eyelids start to drop.

"I agree. I too am yet to see the drawbacks."

He yawns.

"No, I don't think we'd best risk this one much longer – not inside anyway," he says shaking himself awake.

"Still of use, yes, for a time at least."

He frantically goes to work on another cracker.

"No, no point cleaving off any more than is necessary… Yes, too early to tell at this stage."

He brushes the lunch debris off his lap and stands up. He walks over to an oval window and peeks out.

"A sublime irony indeed. It's perfection: petrified of being governed by anything but their own minds, they fail to see the very structure of their own minds as externally governed."

He walks across the room to the other window and creeps one eye out across the glass.

"Quite! The desperation to maintain and protect the very thing that they are protecting against – elegant, truly elegant."

He returns to his seat, but remains perched on the edge.

○

Nolan doesn't see his tails as he returns to his car, but that no longer convinces him that they aren't there. He feels so conspicuous that he's not sure he can even tell the difference anymore.

Best to suspect everything and everyone, sight itself, easier that way, he thinks. Look at Grice's sister and her acolytes. Even Jen's eyes are in the employ of invisible men.

He starts the car and slams his foot down on the accelerator. His back wheels fight for traction before propelling the car in a snake-like motion up the road.

Up ahead there are people crossing: a group of well-dressed women with shopping bags laughing at one another's extravagance, two teenage boys taking it in turns to punch each other on the arm, and a business man in an expensive but crumpled suit gazing ahead as if he were being beckoned by ghosts.

The rest stop short of the car's path, or else clear it by an inch or two, but the business man is not so fortunate. The front bumper obliterates his left knee, shatters the tibia and fibula, and sends the whole lower leg round in the air like a propeller.

Nolan had made no effort to avoid any of the pedestrians, and is now oblivious to having just decimated a man's leg. Aside from the additional drag, he would have been equally unperturbed had he managed to do for the lot.

He has one thing on his mind, and that thing is Smithson. The possibility of salvation is slipping from him, and the only thing replacing it is Smithson's fat face.

A blue light flashes up on the dashboard: a squad vehicle has the lock on him. Three cars back he can see the lights approaching. Pointless attempting the outrun when the lock is on: the pursuing vehicle cannot be shrugged off; the only way to separate the two cars once the lock is initiated is after the inevitable physical unison has been secured.

Possible escape now limited to throwing himself out of the car while it's still moving, Nolan pulls over on the shoulder and slows down. He needs his car to get to Smithson while he still can, so abandoning it is not an option. He has new options now, but he takes no pleasure in them; he'd always wanted his options to have more to them, to be more than what they were: paltry and fleeting deviations from the trajectory of his demise.

The car jolts slightly as the front bumper of the squad car unites with Nolan's back bumper. He now has no control of the vehicle, the squad car's engagement having disabled all independent function.

The patrolman's voice issues from the speakers in Nolan's car, "Are you the owner of this vehicle?"

"Yes," replies Nolan.

"This is an unfortunate situation, Agent Nolan, but you are responsible for a serious road traffic violation within the confines of the Safe Area. I had no choice but to instigate due measure."

"I understand."

"I trust we can we fulfil procedure in a manner more befitting of two colleagues?"

"Of course," says Nolan, sounding duly contrite.

As a sign of goodwill the patrolman reinstates window and door control to Nolan's car, opens his door and steps out.

Nolan drops the window and offers up his ID as the patrolman comes alongside the driver's door.

As the patrolman reaches to take the ID, Nolan swings his left arm across his chest and shoots him in the face.

The patrolman plunges to the tarmac, his legs dancing a joyless jig hopelessly out of time with the monotonous music of the passing cars.

Nolan steps out of his car and moves back toward the open door of the squad car, his louring pixel-flesh eyes scanning the rigid and passive faces of the other road users.

Sitting inside the squad car, Nolan disengages the lock. He waits for the car to fall back, gets out and makes his way to its boot. After a brief rummage he lifts out a grey oblong box, and transfers it to his own boot.

As he is driving away he catches sight of the dead patrolman in his wing mirror. His head has bled out in the shape of a crescent moon. He looks away, but the image of the blood stays put. As he alters the direction of his gaze the image recurs until eventually his entire field of vision is cloaked in an interlacement of haemic sickle blades.

He eases his foot off the accelerator, and holds the steering wheel still, preventing even the slightest rotation. He's on a long straight road, and figures he can manage a minute, maybe two, before he hits something. He also figures that the quickest way to clear his vision would be to crash: a crash will attract the squad cars and he will attract the attention of their occupants; once captured, the modification, having served its purpose – presuming that that's its purpose, or that the affliction even has one – would, he imagined, cease. But he is not certain; and even if he were, the method is somewhat self-defeating.

He manages to travel a mile or more without incident. But, with his vision showing no sign of clearing, frustration takes over and he starts smashing at the sanguinary patchwork of his face panels. After a few initial thumps he starts to concentrate on the eye segments, tapping and scratching at them with his metallic left hand.

A chink in the red blooms in his right eye and then withers into nothing. His fingers become frantic until a crack is formed; the attenuated rupture in the patrolman's lingering blood offers up nothing close to normal vision, but still it is enough for Nolan to continue, to avoid obvious hazards, and successfully negotiate his route to Lab South5.

Smithson, now pacing the room, initiates communication with lab security.

"Do we have him?"

"No word yet, sir."

"I need to know the moment he's picked up."

"As soon as we hear…"

"Who's on the gate?"

"There are four of us on the entrance, sir, but he won't get this far. He'll be flat 'n' strapped before he gets in here."

"You hear anything at all and I want to know about it."

"You'll be informed immediately, sir."

"I'd better be."

Wary of the possibility of additional security, Nolan abandons his car a quarter-mile short of the lab. He takes the long black bag from the boot, and then proceeds to push the car into a ditch by the side of the road.

Access points to the labs' supply tunnels are invariably left unguarded, as any security measures are implemented at point of entry, where each tunnel connects with a lab's storage facility. After climbing down off the road and weaving his way through various concrete hoardings, Nolan finds that today is no exception and that the elevator is unmarked, enabling him to slip inside the supply tunnel unchallenged.

Once inside, still unsure as to whether he has been seen accessing the tunnel, his limited vision preventing him from properly surveying his surroundings, he starts trying to locate a suitable canister. After an excruciatingly long wait, Nolan finally finds a large rapid-access canister, and immediately excavates it from the conduit. He breaks the seal holding the lid down, and empties it of its contents (test tubes, cool boxes, vials, etc.), dumps his bag inside and climbs in after it, neglecting to replace the lid.

Nolan knows that once he reattaches the lid the canister will be airtight. He also knows that the security system will command that the canister collapse in on itself if the lid is not sealed in place, crushing into minimum mass whatever is inside. The machinery only allows closed regulation-canisters to pass into a lab's storage area. The sealed canisters are bomb-proof, and are quarantined for a period sufficient to see out the capacity of any artificial respiration systems that might be employed by a potential interloper. Security can afford to be lax on the outskirts, allowing deliveries to run smoothly and efficiently, because where it matters, where a lab breach is at stake, the conditions are in place to recognise and annihilate any potential threats that might have infiltrated the tunnels. But in addition to all this, Nolan also knows that it is expedient for certain deliveries to evade quarantine, and that where the contents of certain canisters are considered urgent there is a procedure in place to recognise and segregate such containers. All establishments of significance, from the labs to each block of Sceptre Field Park, are eager to maintain the secrecy of their particular procedure and even that they have one in operation at all.

Getting hold of some canned air was not a problem for anyone, and for Nolan easier still, as squad cars, unmarked or otherwise, had them fitted in the boot as standard: the frequency of underground criminality resulting in conflagration was such that, though not a regular occurrence, it was nevertheless considered prudent to equip all law enforcement with the requisite equipment.

Knowledge of how to cheat intake security measures was not so readily available, and Nolan's being privy to it came with the job. That said, Nolan is still beginning to feel the general encroachment of the seemingly coincidental, for although suction pads were also fairly common in police vehicles (offering supplementary control should the main target-and-lock device falter, among other things), he didn't carry them in his car. He'd taken the set now stashed in his black bag from the boot of the dead patrolman's car, and this worried him.

Had he not began to realise the inherent precariousness of his position, regardless of what action he decided to take, he might have started second-guessing himself into some apoplectic spasm of indecision. Instead, he unzips the bag and prepares its contents for use.

As Nolan pulls the lid across the top of the canister he sees the lights in the chamber change from blue to orange, indicating that he is nearing the entrance to Lab South5's storage dock. His face screens lighting the confines of the container, Nolan detaches the mask from the end of the oxygen canister and inserts the pipe directly into his neck. He attaches one suction pad to the floor of the canister and another to the inside of the lid, connects them with the digital ratchet device and watches as it begins drawing them closer together. When the ratchet device stops – having sensed the optimum pressure level before incurring damage to the surfaces to which it is attached – Nolan checks that the lid is secure by slamming his palms into it as hard as he can.

He detects no movement.

Nolan is still taking a risk and he knows it: there is no guarantee that the system has not been modified, that the broken seal will now not draw more attention as a result of those modifications, regardless of how securely the lid is in place; and even if the cracked seal is not picked up on, recovery times, even of urgent canisters, can still differ considerably depending on volume, leaving Nolan to suffocate inside before ever gaining access to the storage facility. But feeling the full weight of the odds stacked against him, and having no other means of getting his hands on Smithson, Nolan puts these concerns from his mind.

As he curls up around his weapon, he feels his mind being dragged back to the last time he'd folded himself up in a confined space to avoid detection.

Back in the issue greys, seams carving up his limbs, cuffs stiff as bog rolls and collar litzen digging in under the chin like a heretic's fork, Nolan takes one look at the shallow recess in the floor and sets his wattles swinging, "Fuck dyu take me for?"

"There's plenty of room, Nolan; quit your bleating!" says Cokey, Nolan's superior by a single coloured square, shit-eater smirk perming mouth-ends either side of his profoundly acuminate greyhound head.

"You really are a lame cunt."

Cokey pushes his gloved hands deep into the ratty pockets of his charcoal bone sack and shrugs his plated shoulders.

"And you'll be over there," says Nolan pointing to a damaged section of fibreboard panelling on one of the factory's external walls.

"Uh-huh. Measure it if you want; it's no bigger. At least you get to lie down."

"I'm not feeling the privilege."

"We run into the remainder before reinforcements get here and we're screwed. There's not many left, but they're more than us, a lot more. I don't see what else…"

"There'll be lab trucks and grunts all over this place in less than an hour, so crawling into the floor and the walls don't exactly strike me as necessary. It's them that wanna be hiding."

"And when they do, it'll be somewhere like here, and seeing that they're caught in a shrinking circle who's to say it won't be here."

"You're pretty pessimistic for a guy spends most of his time falling outta planes."

"Pessimism's got fuck all to do with it. We hide and we can relax; we can buy ourselves some time and, if need be, the potential for a shock assault."

"What? Wait! Here it comes. Shit. Can you believe they think it fucking needful to remind me of your rank?" Nolan sidles up to Cokey and curtseys.

"Saves me having to do it," says Cokey, only half-joking.

"The sooner these fuckers are done running the better; who needs this shit going off in their head."

"Careful, Nolan! Let's not forget what your brain, infinitesimal as it is, would look like if you'd brought it along for the ride."

"As chewed up as your shitter, so the story goes."

"You'd have more in there than the odd protocol nudge, that's for sure."

"So the story goes."

"You saw the encephalic honeycomb on initiation."

"Yep, and I ain't seen one since."

"And that disappoints you? What, you think they buried that poor sod's brain in the ground and let the worms mistake it for mud?"

"No, I believe an invisible airborne plague devoured it like it's devoured the brains of Schismatists all over, and that they are determined to perpetuate its spread, but the fact that I believe it don't make it true. It's an explanation, but how can I be sure it's the best one?"

"So you'd be happy to risk ending up like them just to satisfy your curiosity?"

"That's the problem: I'm not sure I can see anything wrong with them."

"You've heard what they believe, what they do."

"Heard but not seen. All I see is people running and fighting in panic. They think we're murderers. It's not until the shot's in them that they lose that look in their eyes, like they've seen..."

"It's just the heads. That's what they're designed to do. They're fine once they've been through the labs. You've seen them afterwards; you've fought alongside them; you can't possibly deny the improvement."

"The fear's gone," says Nolan, his tone unequivocal.

"They repair the damage. It's the damage that makes them run and fight in the first place."

"All of a sudden that hole in the floor is looking a lot more appealing."

"Don't let me stop you."

Nolan climbs down into the shallow trench, lays his weapon alongside him and starts dragging some spare fibreboards over the top of him. "Wake me in Spring," he says as Cokey slides the last board into place over the hyphenated yellow ovals of his eyes.

Cokey takes one last look out onto the street. It is bereft of life: the only thing he can see that had once laid claim to a heartbeat is the mangled corpse of one of the Schismatist's cats.

They keep those things in their homes, and Nolan can't see anything wrong with them, he thinks, fucking guy wants looking at.

He can hear the rumbling of the mobile labs in the distance, and wonders if Nolan hadn't been right about there being no need to hide this close to the end. But with Nolan already interred, he sides with caution and proceeds to sepulchre himself in the wall. The cavity is the result of some clumsy pipe removal: instead of filling the now defunct space they'd simply left it. They'd even done a hack job on the fibreboard panel, which means it is easy for Cokey to prise away from the studwork and then pull back into position.

All the while the factory remains empty Nolan has no problem keeping his breathing under control; he can fidget at will, and he knows that if he starts sweating the confinement too much he can always dislodge the top board for a few minutes to calm his nerves. But all this changes when fifteen Schismatist combatants happen upon the factory.

They've been concealed in their incommodious sanctums for about half an hour when they turn up.

The moment when Nolan and Cokey first hear the metal

shutter roll up they both hope, laced with a certain amount of presumption, that it is their own men, but nevertheless they stay put, neither of them relishing the ignominy of being seen excavating themselves from their hideaways like craven mice. Their reluctance is rewarded on hearing their visitors talking in that unmistakeably Schismatic argot.

"Is there safety here?" asks a lad of about fifteen, his bottom lip cut and puffy, carrying a fat tabby cat, its legs hanging flaccid then stiffening from a dream.

"There is resistance and a fated brush," says a woman of an age to be his mother. "The safety spoken of might imply unmentioned things."

"The windows will have eyes on the inside," says a flint-faced man wearing the still, execrable eyes of a basilisk, as he points out positions to various men and women, the top half of their heads mantled with black beanies, who scurry obediently into place.

Nolan is feeling it; his brain not only seeming to be inside his discrepant bovid skull, but doing its best to burst its way out. Cokey is faring better, due in no small part to his being able to observe through a slim crack in the fibreboard the movements of his enemy, and so train his weapon on any that happen to approach his location.

"There'll be resting and the consumption of food in shifts," says the man given to making orders.

Six beanie-heads man the windows, their heads flicking to

and fro like prairie dogs, while the rest of them sit in a corner with two stretchered bodies and eat from tins and silver packets.

"Will food nourish where it is not taken?" asks the boy.

"Rest will be nourishment enough for now," replies an old man massaging the phlebitis in his calves.

"There needs to be trust that that comment wasn't in any way greed-related," says a thin man dressed in denim and missing a hand.

"That trust is deserved; it's been earned," replies the old man.

"What is it exactly that's deserving of trust?" asks the woman of an age to be the boy's mother.

The thin man lets out a malefic titter.

The old man stares down at his blown veins and fights against the profanity that is shame.

"Of the ways to disappear this is currently among the least useful," says the man given to orders through a mouthful of food.

"There is truth," says the thin man.

"Where there should be silence," is the peremptory man's response.

And noiselessness is observed by all.

Nolan longs for them to resume their aimless bickering, thus allowing him the opportunity to make minute adjustments in his limbs, which serves to stave off cramp and help divert his attention away from the vulnerability of his predicament. He feels every second of his body's inertness.

Dreams of Amputation

Ten minutes pass without noise or incident.

Once again Cokey has an easier time, for he has sensed a growing unease in the beanie-heads at the windows. Their movements have become progressively twitchy, and their glances back at the seated group more frequent.

"Contaminants!" says a woman at a north-facing window.

Those located on the east and west walls echo her warning.

With the south-facing wall offering no means of observation or exit they are effectively surrounded.

Both Nolan and Cokey celebrate with a deep draw of air.

"The building will be rigged as is keeping with non-acquiescence," says the peremptory man.

Nolan and Cokey cut short their celebration.

"An absence of coercion should be heard as truth," says the woman of an age to be the boy's mother.

The boy looks at her. The woman looks at him.

"As it has been," says the old man, unzipping a green satchel.

The beanie-heads gather round and the old man hands out a small device to each one of them, which they handle gingerly.

The boy becomes increasingly restless.

"Time needs to be allocated," says the woman.

"There's all the time till it's done," says a beanie-head returning to her lookout.

Certain that nobody but the boy is watching her, the woman mouths the word 'Go'.

He gets to his feet and starts backing towards the exit. His eyes do not stray from hers.

"Come with me!" he screams at her.

She looks away as everyone else glowers in his direction.

"Infection!" hollers the old man.

"I'm sorry. I'm scared. Don't stay here! Please don't stay here. I…" The boy stops moving and scans their faces.

Thirteen guns are trained on his head.

The woman of that age hides her eyes in her lap, shaking.

"If the infection is still present after ten it will be eradicated," says the peremptory man.

"Mum!" he roars, his vision befogged with tears.

"Ten, nine, eight…" all but the mother count in concert.

The boy runs for the shutter, slides it up just far enough to scramble underneath, and is out on the street as they count off the number three.

One of the beanie-heads rolls the shutter back down to the floor, and they all resume the various tasks allotted to them by circumstance: to watch, to defend, to cease.

The thin man shakes his head. "All that time running and…"

"And what?" says the mother without raising her head.

"And the contagion was in attendance," the thin man continues.

Cokey has used the distraction to push the wall panel out enough to enable him to turn around and hold his rifle horizontally. As the commotion ends he is facing the raw block work that separates him from the street.

Dreams of Amputation

Nolan too has made use of the cover. He's dislodged one of the boards across his face, so that he can see out. Although the board isn't raised up far, he is still running the risk of being spotted. But then if he is going to have a chance of evading the explosion he is going to have to do something. He figures he has a few minutes before the reinforcements make the Schismatist's position untenable. Lifting the board an inch or two more, he can see the lump that has formed recently in the wall where Cokey is holed up.

He's going to move any moment, he thinks. Cokey is obviously in the best position to initiate an assault, so Nolan decides to give him a couple of minutes to do just that, at which time he will hasten a resolution alongside him.

Nolan has counted off thirty of one-twenty when he hears Cokey's gun blasting. He is about to burst free of the floor when he hesitates.

Cokey is still nowhere to be seen, and neither are the effects of his gunshots. The only difference Nolan can see are the bursts of yellow fog emitting from the cracks in the wall.

The Schismatists all look on, stupefied, their feet slowly shuffling them backwards.

Nolan begins to extricate himself from what he feels sure is only a few minutes away from becoming his grave should he remain immobile.

The gunshots end.

Nolan crawls across the uneven floor to an upturned workbench, its six legs splayed and bent protruding skyward like a dead insect.

After the dust has cleared a female beanie-head approaches the damaged section of wall. She smashes the loose wall panel free from its housings and steps back as the wet night air washes in through a ragged hole in the block-work. She rushes to re-place the panel, and two others are quick to assist her.

Having reached the workbench, Nolan makes use of the sudden efflux of communication, loud and perfervid, amongst the Schismatists, and pulls the workbench up onto its side, shielding himself behind it.

They are going to blow the place at any moment. About that Nolan has no doubt. The gunfire and the subsequent discovery of the hole in the wall have rattled them. They sense that the ability to control their fates is slipping away fast, and they have no intention of submitting to capture. They begin to charge their devices.

Lying flat to the ground, all but his head and the barrel of his rifle hidden behind the workbench, Nolan aims at the pe-remptory man and fires. The shot hits him just below the left ear and explodes on impact; his head, neck and right shoulder disin-tegrate in an instant, returning to the eye as a piece of Pointillist sculpture scattered across the faces and bodies of his comrades.

Nolan takes out two more before any of them are in a posi-tion to return fire. As he rolls back behind the worktop he hears a voice from outside demanding immediate capitulation; a voice so stentorian as to drown out the report of their weapons.

Sensation of extreme heat in his left thigh.

Silence.

White burn of magnesium sun.

…

Black tang of star-scrubbed night.

One of the Schismatists had detonated his device in error, killing himself and all but one of his comrades – who though incapacitated didn't die until two days later – with an immediacy that prevented any of the others from detonating their own devices. This man's ineptitude saved Nolan's life. Had all the devices gone off they would certainly have bitten a chunk out of the earth that would have included not only Nolan, but the entire factory and a good portion of its neighbour as well.

Nolan did not escape without injury, but he escaped – with the memory of who had escaped before him, at his expense, intact.

Oxygen is nearly out. The canister is still in motion, and all the while it remains that way Nolan cannot disengage the suction pads, for only once the canister has stopped is it safe to open the lid, for only then is it likely to be inside the express area of the storage facility. Avoiding being crushed on entry was only one half of the problem, and now he faces the second half and all he can do is wait. If he releases the pads before he reaches the express area the canister will be detected, resealed and diverted into the hermetic long-term quarantine unit; the canister will no longer be commanded to collapse in on itself, as is the case with the perimeter defences, but the consequences for Nolan would be equally grave, so he must wait until the canister stops, however desperate he is to do otherwise.

Nolan's limbs are jerking violently, his elbows and knees crashing into the sides of the canister as he starts to lose control. His chest starts heaving as he gulps for air, all thoughts and mental images expiring into the void of gradual asphyxiation.

He senses a change in momentum.

The canister's stopped! he thinks. He can't sense any movement, but he's not sure he's in a position to tell anymore. He's not sure that his need hasn't erroneously convinced him of its truth.

He hesitates.

Still not knowing, and sensing that the time has passed when such knowledge is possible, he hits the release button on the ratchet device, pushes decompress on the top pad and kicks the lid off with his feet.

The lid flies up in the air and as he watches it revolve in the blue light he grabs for his weapon and scrambles into a kneeling position, his neck open, pulsating, his already diminished vision now murky and inconstant.

Hearing nothing but the whirring of machinery, he guesses

his breach of the canister has so far gone undetected. He crouches back down inside and waits for his vision to improve. When he looks again a white-smocked lab porter is standing alongside the canister looking right at him through slatted chrome goggles.

Nolan lets off a blast without bothering to correct his aim. A fuzz of metal issues from the barrel, half of which catches the lab porter in the neck. His head slumps into his right shoulder and slides down his back onto the floor: a snowman melting in the sun. It is not until Nolan has clambered free of the canister and collided with it while making his exit that the headless body finally topples over.

Nolan is quick to remove himself from the main intake area, and after following numerous narrow corridors, each of which is punctuated with many unnumbered, windowless doors, he enters a corridor wider than the rest, at the end of which is an elevator. He runs towards it.

As he closes in on the elevator its doors part, revealing a scientist from the labs upstairs and another porter.

Without slowing down, Nolan fires a shot from waist height which rips through their stomachs. They stand in the entrance to the elevator looking down at their mutilated midriffs, more confounded than terror-struck. As Nolan barges through the middle of them they spill all over the marble floor, and he is forced to shove their remains out of the way with his foot to stop the elevator doors from jamming.

He rides the elevator to the ground floor, his gun trained on the doors all the way up.

The doors open on the western end of Lab South5. Directly in front of him he can see the main lab complex, and to his left the first of ten white cubes. Without being certain which of these offers the best chance of finding Smithson, he instinctually finds himself heading in the direction of the main lab complex, and being distrustful of the force of this completely groundless conviction, he corrects his route, heading off instead in the direction of the living quarters.

There's a clear path to Smithson's block. Nolan sprints toward it, the enflamed undercarriage of the sky mirroring his progress. As he places his palm on the white wall, he sees a suited figure reflected in the window.

Nolan's unborn skin flickers as the first blow completes its arched descent. His legs sag momentarily from the hips. Three more blows put him on his knees. His upper half stoops into the jagged shale as they drag him back to the main body of the lab.

The haphazard ballet of airborne rubbish is virtually the only thing on the road as Grice enters District 14. His sister's apartment is in a now nameless complex on the border between Districts 14 and 15. He can't stand living there anymore. He can't stay there any longer and watch and attempt to nurture the atrophied wreckage of her personality. It has to end, and any end is preferable to its continuance. While he still has a memory of what she once was he will have to act. He has accepted this. He can't have his image of her completely eaten away by what she has become. Her condition is corrosive.

The main reason he had not ventured to think such thoughts before now was the miraculous change in all those people at Sybaris6, who all of a sudden returned to normal. This could happen to her, he would think. One day she will be back, and she will stay that way. He'll take her to his place on the lake and keep her away from the city. But a call had come through that morning that effaced all traces of that already fading and increasingly tattered hope.

("This Grice, 53rd precinct?"

"Yep. Who's this?"

"You're on my contact list. I'm the concierge over at Sybaris6. It's happened again.")

Regret was quickly displaced by resolve, but as the day went on he felt with a terrible clarity the swamping gloom of all that that resolution represented, for him and for the life he was supposed to continue living.

Down every street he turns there are faces at windows looking out into the grey evening, watching his car pass through with eyes, like his sister's, occupied at a distance.

Grice tries to remember his parents before the disease hit, and with those shoddy remnants wishes them back to act as final consuls on what he plans to do. Grice's mother and father both succumbed in the same month, within a week of each other. It took little more than six weeks for it to eat their souls.

An earlier version of this disease, which was considerably slower in its annihilation of persons, used to go by the name Alzheimer's. Thariasun's Syndrome (named after its discoverer, American physician Peter Thariasun), the name given to this more aggressive variant, could reduce healthy adults, usually over the age of fifty (fifteen years earlier than the danger age of Alzheimer's), to raisin-brained inanimates in a matter of a few weeks. Like all victims of Thariasun's, Grice's parents had no time to make provision for their escape, to commit suicide, or ask for assistance that would lead to a quick release. It hits the language function first (consuming more or less the entire area around the sylvian fissure), and then moves on to target the motor skills, invariably just the arms (much like a localised Parkinson's), so that within hours the sufferer is unable to communicate even the most basic of thoughts.

Grice had been so devastated by the eradication of his parents that he had gone to considerable effort to visit Dr. Thariasun. At that time Thariasun was based in a lab located within an entirely different Region to the one in which Grice lived. Travelling between Regions was not easy, and it had taken almost a year to arrange a ten minute face-to-face conversation. Thariasun was eccentric in his refusal to use artificial communication systems for anything but the most basic of tasks. He didn't trust them. He remained to be convinced that the increasingly wide-spread network of virtually interconnected minds was even benign, let alone beneficial. If it hadn't been for the prominence of much of his early work as a physician, the bizarre nature of some of his beliefs would have attracted negative attention much sooner than it did.

One thing Thariasun had said during those ten minutes granted to Grice had resonated with him ever since. At that stage in his career Thariasun was still rather cagey when it came to his theoretical speculations, and it wasn't until much later that he felt compelled to share his various hypotheses with the scientific community at large, but nevertheless he had hinted at what was to come in a closing remark that Grice could not forget and could not dismiss, as most tried their hardest to do to a number of unpublished papers, circulated ten years later, in which Thariasan expanded on the same idea.

A significant portion of Grice's audience with Thariasun had been spent discussing the details of his parent's case, with Thariasun assuring Grice, on more than one occasion, that his absence during the first few days of them displaying signs of the Syndrome could have had no effect on the eventual outcome whatsoever. His parent's demise was all too typical, the end all too inevitable. Then, as their ten minutes was coming to a close, Grice asked him what it was that had made both his parents particularly susceptible when they seemed so very different in their habits and temperament. Grice could still remember how the

Dr's face became almost numinous as he contemplated his answer. He said that however peculiar it sounded he still could not rule out contagion. The significance of this remark had passed him by at the time, and he had simply shaken his head and lamented the utter pointlessness of what his parents had endured. It was Thariasun's response to this, the last words he ever spoke to Grice, that refused to slip away into the forever-muted jumble of long-lost dialogue. He said, with a seriousness unmatched by anything he'd said in the nine and three-quarter minutes before, "Interests are being served. Be sure of it. If it looks pointless you're thinking too small." Grice wasn't sure that he wasn't still thinking too small, that he'd never be able to think big enough to truly grasp the meaning of Thariasun's words. But regardless of all he couldn't see, all the minutiae he'd never be privy to, he could no longer fail to act on the truth he did perceive, in those words, in those words in his sister.

Grice put his proposal to his half-remembered parents, and imagined them consenting. He was unable to have them muster even the most rudimentary of reservations. Either he'd appropriated their faces as his own, filled their intangible skins with requirements instead of memories, or else the situation was as clear as it seemed and options for resolution were indeed as limited as he thought them to be.

As he pulls into the open-air car park surrounding his sister's apartment block he looks up and sees a gridded mass of obnubilated faces sliding back into the darkness of their rooms.

Some lights come on. He sees shadows shrink and swell across white walls. The car park is deserted. Most of the cars haven't moved in weeks. Grice is reluctant to open his door, to leave his car and go inside. He wonders how far this reluctance extends into his future. He can see no end to it. Panicking, his hands fumbling and slippery, he exits his car as quickly as he can and heads for the elevator. Once inside he leans his back up against the mirrored wall and relaxes slightly.

As the doors open onto his floor, his breathing is even and his palms are dry. His composure regained, he steps out into the hallway and walks slowly and assuredly past door after door until he reaches his sister's. Once inside, he stops, his head turning from side to side as if searching out a prompt. Seeing the door to the living room is open he goes inside and takes off his jacket. He throws it onto the table where his sister is sitting. She does not acknowledge his arrival in any way; remaining perfectly still, she stares out of the window, her right hand placed across a slim pile of paper, the top sheet of which is crammed with tiny scribbled notations.

Grice does not look at her. He places his hand on his gun, and looks around the room absentmindedly. He lingers on certain items, his face quizzical, as if he is trying to place them within the context of the room. He walks into the small kitchen area and pours himself a glass of water. As he returns to the living room he takes careful sips from his drink. He sits down on the sofa and places the glass on a low table in front of him. The lineation of his face reveals a relaxed state of confusion, an easy befuddlement that gradually, over the course of the next hour, degrades into stupor.

●

Smithson and his two associates stand over Nolan and wait for him to return to full consciousness.

"The unsanctioned voice of incompleteness always fades in translation. The stolen baby has already imploded. His code is being monitored at various intersections, its formless circuits sucked back into the master configuration." Smithson scratches at his buttoned gut as he looks down into the smoky, nictitating snow of Nolan's face. "Time to wake up, Agent Nolan."

When Nolan comes to he is unable to move. His eyes remain closed; he doubts the mechanisms and their screens are there to open. He senses a presence but there is no noise. He waits for the world to return.

"Now, now, agent Nolan, tears, you really mustn't do it to yourself. Anything dug from a cunt wants distraction. The fluke don't discriminate. Even that shit out there we have you sweep up knows there ain't nobody crawls free of the game."

Attempting to move, Nolan finds his hands and legs bound to a reclining chair, and a neck brace restricting all head movement.

"You'll regret this."

"And why's that? You really must try to keep up. You're obsolete, Agent Nolan. We can process them now. We've been able to for some time." Smithson twists his neck in the direction of the viewless window. "The terror is over up here. The H-Belt secures that purpose now: it maps itself and leaks in measured and controllable doses. Undigested dread sold to entertainment conglomerates for huge sums and then piped out into the world – snarling organs of a greater beast, precision-engineered brutalization ensuring all of our futures, maintaining the balance, keeping us sane."

"Hell..."

"That's one name for it. Everything serves a purpose, even those recalcitrant nobodies festering in The Tubes' hidden district which, incidentally, is where you're destined to end up."

"Where else."

"Don't be so defeatist. This is a victory for you. There's no other way."

"You want gratitude?"

"Anyway, we must press on. But before we begin there's something I must confess."

"I'm not interested."

"Oh I think you will be. Although, I don't think you'll approve. You see, I had someone arrange me another visit."

Nolan stares up at the ceiling and tries to block out Smithson's voice.

"Can you guess who I chose? I bet you can."

Nolan closes his eyes.

"I thought so. Their flesh is like blossom on a dead tree. She is no different. Grice set it up. He could see you were weakening. But I can understand now why you'd go to such lengths to keep her."

"Grice wouldn't…"

"Grice wouldn't what? Try not to be quite such a moron, Nolan. Grice does whatever needs to be done, same as you, same as me, same as every fucking thing on this sorry-arsed planet."

"Maybe."

"The world's a shuffling horde trademarked with decay. There are no techniques; everything gets devoured – even you. Private space on any other terms but these is a dreary little dream. Time to wake up, Nolan. Time to wake up."

"The others. What about the others."

"What others?"

"He mentioned them over and over. Others, like him, trying to get out. I saw the files. I went to the container and took them."

"I'm sorry, you're mistaken."

"No. No I'm not. I can show you them."

"By all means." Smithson flips his palms skyward.

"I understand: wringing it dry before it's gone."

"Just a little joke."

"You should train your Capuchins better. They're not laughing."

"Anyway, I thank you for your generous offer, but we already have them."

"Then you know."

"I know what isolation does. It does what isolation always does, what it always has done: it creates company."

"Sages don't make mistakes."

"Sages are gifted with universal knowledge. How they end up utilizing that knowledge is dependent on other factors, human factors. The universality of their knowledge is not on-going. Following the procedure there is always room for interpretation of incoming evidence, for deviation, for human weakness."

"But his desires were modelled on mine. Unless you..."

"Not everything's a lie – what would be the point?"

"So..."

"So like you he started to dream. But he got carried away, started imagining he could slip free of the Horde itself, saw things that weren't there: a way out, salvation. We were as interested as you to see where he'd go. The only difference was we knew there was nowhere for him to go, nowhere outside of this, anyhow."

"This?"

"This. All of this. But then you must have suspected that."

"Suspected what?"

"But I suppose all you were interested in was getting someone on whom you could test your hypothesis – an hypothesis that we allowed you to find – and who better than a Sage, right? And then he went and disappeared before you could assess the results and have him fill you in on anything you might have missed, from the inside. Most unfortunate. The process takes its toll as you know, but rest assured he is still functioning; you saw that for yourself."

"What did he see?"

"What he thought he saw was a breach in The Horde, a conceptual rip that he could wriggle out through. After you lost contact he was busy paring himself down, stripping his self of its trappings bit by bit."

"So ZS1 was what, a figment of his imagination?"

"A delusory entity; the product of his distorted hopes, yes."

"You're certain?"

"Completely."

"No such thing."

"As complete as I need to be."

"And the Horde? Just more of the same?"

"The Horde Self is no extrapolation. It's the reason for everything. The reason we're here now. The reason you are going where you are going and have been where you've been."

"Sounds like someone's found God."

"In a manner of speaking."

"Some God."

"Well today he is going to grant your wish, Agent Nolan. You are going to be set free from the mainframe. But as I've already mentioned, there is a price."

"Always a price."

"I'm afraid so. It's the only place where disconnection is permitted, the only place where it makes any sense."

"Sense? Have you been there?"

"No. I wouldn't be here talking to you now if I had. You've seen what happens to those who only slightly exceed the recommended exposure, let alone those that enter the place."

"You're talking about Harshaw."

"Yes. He's a state isn't he?"

"One last twist?"

"Just stating facts, Agent Nolan. None of this is in my hands. You must understand that."

"All right, turn the fucking screen on! Let's get this over with."

"I sense you're tiring of our little chat. I won't keep you any longer." Smithson nods to one of his associates, who makes some last-minute adjustments to the screen.

"If I ever get out of there…"

"You won't."

"We'll see. Best pray I don't."

"Anyway, you'll be too busy to worry about me. Don't torture yourself. It was never going to end any other way."

"Are you ready yet?"

"Okay?"

Smithson's associate nods his head, his finger poised over a white keyboard.

"I hope it's everything you hoped it'd be."

Nolan stares into the screen.

"Okay, run it!"

The mucilaginous reassurances of the jelly mass made dull symptom. The HORDE – soft-walled, murderous, stuck together with masticated souls – always wins, and this is no exception.

"Okay, transfer him. He's done" says Smithson as he waddles over to his desk and starts tucking into an iced donut.

Nolan's limp body is wheeled out into the hallway.

Nolan's head slips from the concrete step onto the one below, bringing him round immediately. He sits up and surveys his surroundings: a disused stairwell, its lower steps hidden beneath a swell of all manner of foul-smelling detritus.

He hears shrieks from the floor above, and smells the stench of boiling intestines coming through the walls, putrid onslaught of steatorrhoeaic junk-food shit.

There's a squeaking noise coming from the floor above, sound of a field mouse in mortal distress. He pushes himself up onto his legs. As he climbs the steps he digs his fingertips into the soft plaster of the walls to steady himself.

Turning the corner on the landing above he sees an extremely thin man dressed in blue overalls. He immediately recognizes the man as Johnny Jr., his absent Sage.

"Hey!" shouts Nolan.

The Sage carries on walking. He doesn't appear to have heard Nolan, or if he has is utterly unfazed by his presence. Nolan comes up alongside him and taps him on the arm.

The Sage turns to him, his face cut with concentration.

He speaks: "The future's in confinement – restricted, pointless. They've exhausted its possibilities, making it their greatest enemy, left disembodied in their own hereafter of choked possibilities and perverted salesmen charismatic to the last, with nothing to sell but their threadbare ends…"

"Slow down!" says Nolan.

"Not possible. Have to get it out before it consumes me. Got to keep processing it before it processes me. Can't stop. Got to keep moving it on."

"We have to get out of here. Is there any way out?"

"There are minds here of manifest delusions, transcending themselves at every turn, shattering identities – mutilated echoes of the maggot-marrowed bones of empty wonder. The code of the gaps is a persuasive fiction, but it's infected with bugs. My past slid down the window like unwanted scenery. I let it go."

"I don't… What are you saying?"

"Empty circles of scrambled hope continually sucked down into this quicksand of network silence. Billions of sick minds churning out legions of parasitic worms ailing for new flesh, crawling around inside a thousand internal voices, processing them into the hibernation of all human narrative."

"Listen to me! Is there any way out of here? If we work together maybe we can…"

"This place has done for me; I'm inside these walls, out in unbound worlds, away from all diluted carriers and scrambled myths. It's a bleak purpose I observe, these techniques in rotting. I'm a nursemaid to stillborns, an operative of some relentless blackening. I maintain the temperature, regurgitate my eyes as stylized chunks of horror. I reorganize all of it. I can't just leave them as they are. I can't. What would it mean to leave them as they are? Like this?"

"Fuck em! We need to find a way out. What the… Are you listening to me? We need to get the fuck out." Nolan grabs hold of the Sage's arm.

"I've found my way out. This is my way out. You need to find yours, if you haven't found it already."

A way out… The stillness in his head; he'd been so distracted he hadn't even noticed. Finally he could lay claim to every thought, intrusive or otherwise. He is free. His location slips from his consciousness for a moment as he revels in his internal quietude. Even there in the Belt there's relief. The sacrifices have been too many, but… He decides it best not to think of Jenny. Not yet.

"I think something has happened," he eventually replies.

"You won't last long up here. I can help you."

"There are safe areas?"

"There are safer areas."

The Sage turns away and walks toward another staircase.

Nolan's ears echo with the retrospective prayers of tens of thousands of time-flattened souls while, what the Sage refers to as, "entropy theorists" replay their experiments to motionless paranoids and decomposing predators, their faces buried in the unreality of illuminated tunnels, tunnels of writhing sleep thick with the memorized sounds of screams spilling from a thousand freshly cut throats.

"Follow me!" says the Sage beginning his descent.

Nolan, strangely unnerved by the sounds, follows without question or hesitation.

Lab cooks with excessively gnawed fingernails pass Nolan on the stairs, complaining of increased exposure to repackaged silence, the tweeting of caged robins, cryptozoological excursions into the soft logarithms of televised consciousness...

Nolan remains within touching distance of the Sage. He knows he needs his help, but it's more than that, for he is somehow comforted by his presence. As he traces the Sage's footfalls he listens to his berserk noise. Noise approximating the shape of words.

"Behind the shroud is a voluptuous fear. We wandering merchants frail from rapid strides and immortal confusion consult this hubbub for sense, these spirits perverse with deformities with rage. Radiant, they purge the air of decay. Our still mutiny will eclipse all wakeful assembly, trample time and the lakes of God's fatal empire. Flowers will bloom like cataracts…"

"Where are we going?" asks Nolan.

"All those brains ransacked, sliding back into a bleached sleep, a sleep owned…"

"Who? Who owns it?"

"Like on death row, routine has become an integral part of the execution process…"

"I don't…"

"This cityscape drips in the artificial habit, from rocking heads fucked open in babbling doorways to bodies wrapped in garbage, their screams weaved into the dead air. Look! There!" He points into a grot-encrusted courtyard to their left, where bodies are stretching and warping like shadows in cheap Polaroid scenes of barbaric fogged morphology.

"There's no explanation for why I'm no longer submersible. Still wake in the wetsuit every morning. Weights in place on the belt. Feet lined in cold lead. And yet no getting under. The others tell me how the mask still fits, explain how it is that no water can get in. Type fingers on its window. And I feel the canister still has air. But the load somehow different now. Lighter than before. I had alibis then. Alibis I could gnaw on when I needed to evidence my teeth. There's not one solid thing left. Every overdrawn breath invents a different exit. Somewhere there's some neat place to drown. I localize and dilute. I scrounge new exertions of claustrophobia. I forgo all instruments of surfacing. But then surfacing's who I am. What I'll have to return to. What I'll think is me when finally I get back under."

"But you got out not under."

"Turns out they can be the same thing."

They head down into a steel-clad underpass housing beet-root-faced barflies wearing piranha smiles slumped into puddles of their own urine, an alien despair munching through their future's weak schedules.

One of them lifts his head up off the floor and regales them as they pass: "Dreaming death-sex n cut flowers nya? Cam on, you can tell me. Don't trust them whores none. They farm insects neath their tongues come out n eat your cock. Hey! You listening?" He waves his arms, each one coated in raw patches the colour and texture of sliced salami.

All Nolan can hear is the Sage: "Clot of masks, of minds dissected by the vehicle of days, of time leaning into its own perpetually shifting dead-end. And up there, nothing but the shrunken insides of externalized surveillance..."

"What are you talking about?" asks Nolan, his face a pixel dream of evening rainfall.

The Sage's eyes remain saccading across the wall in front of him as he replies: "Please don't ask about the reports. I can't answer. Would you ask a man to feed on his own sick?"

They pass abandoned laboratories, chairs and beds still screwed into the concrete floors.

"Behold the true picture of intimacy," says the Sage ushering Nolan to a small window.

Inside is a scrambled female form wrapped in dirty blankets, scarlet mouth spread wide, thick-skinned slug secreting poisoned silver slime across the thighs of her spent attackers.

Nolan is starting to feel nauseous. He rams his hands into his pockets in an attempt to keep them still. The feel of scrunched paper in his right hand. He takes it out and flattens it against his palm.

"What does this say?" says Nolan, excitedly, handing the paper, a mesh of creases and swirling ink, over to the Sage. "It's yours. I found it in your container. You wrote it. Right?"

The Sage nods.

"So what's it say?"

"It's not translatable at the current time."

"But you wrote it."

"I made the marks."

"You wrote it without knowing what it meant?"

"Maybe."

"Maybe?"

"I can't remember. It slid and I let it go."

The Sage turns and climbs through a large pipe into a narrow-gutted alleyway strewn with decaying bodies. Nolan follows, keeping his eyes firmly pinned to the back of his guide's head. He tries his best not to register the smell.

The Sage stops.

"Why have we stopped?" asks Nolan.

"You need to go down there." He points to his right down a dimly-lit alleyway. At the end of the alleyway, Nolan can just make out an open door.

"Where are you going?"

"This way." He points straight ahead. "You need to go that way." He walks off without saying another word.

Nolan, with no real convictions of his own about what he should do or where he should go, follows the Sage's advice and heads toward the open door.

Through the door he finds a small room damp with condensation. There is a large screen on the wall and a heavily padded armchair positioned in front of it. He closes the reinforced door behind him, turns the key in the lock and secures the two arm-sized bolts positioned on the top and the bottom of the door.

Jenny sits, as ever, watching the screens, her fingers tapping, her eyes everywhere at once. Sitting down in the armchair, Nolan lets the image flood his consciousness, blocking out everything else. He can smell her hair, and almost feel its silken weight sliding free of his fingers. He watches the steady swell and shrinkage of her chest, and imagines her warm breath moving across his cheek. He talks and hears his voice echo past her ears. He tells her that he's free to think, that he can enjoy her fully for the first time, without the sense that he's disseminating her wonders far and wide. He relaxes into his new state, reinforcing its confines for fear of destroying it with needs it cannot possibly satisfy.

A red light shines across her face momentarily. Nolan's heart grows legs.

●

The Sage motionless in a piss-swamp arcade, the wall a world to him lost in calenture: the prototypical anhedonian captured in some dark viscid frieze.

He jolts.

Reaches into his pocket.

From a crumpled page, gifted back by Nolan minutes earlier, he reads:

There will always be dreamers. And amputation will always be their dream. I too dream of it, and so the dream becomes my amputation. For that is how I must remove myself; not like them with the entirety of my being, but in parts, slicing and dicing myself into billions upon billions of pieces, and that way forget that I even exist at all. But even my amputation must end.

●

Gary J. Shipley is the author of several books, including Theoretical Animals and Crypt(o)spasm. His work has appeared in Gargoyle, The Black Herald, Glossator, New Dead Families, elimae, >kill author, nthposition, 3:AM, and others. More details can be found at Thek Prosthetics.

YESTERDAY'S NOW

COPELAND VALLEY

FURTHER READING

Your Cities, Your Tombs by Jordan Krall

·

How To Avoid Sex by Matthew Revert

·

Feast of Oblivion by Josh Myers

·

The Doom Magnetic Trilogy by William Pauley III

·

Karaoke Death Squad by Eric Mays

·

Beyond The Valley of the Apocalypse Donkeys by
Jordan Krall

·

The Copeland Valley Sampler by Various

www.copelandvalley.com

CPSIA information can be obtained
at www.ICGtesting.com
Printed in the USA
BVHW031353301118
533936BV00007B/369/P